Weather Permitting
& Other Stories

Essential Prose Series 122

**Canada Council
for the Arts**

**Conseil des Arts
du Canada**

**ONTARIO ARTS COUNCIL
CONSEIL DES ARTS DE L'ONTARIO**
an Ontario government agency
un organisme du gouvernement de l'Ontario

Canadä

Guernica Editions Inc. acknowledges the support of the Canada Council
for the Arts and the Ontario Arts Council. The Ontario Arts Council
is an agency of the Government of Ontario.

We acknowledge the financial support of the Government of Canada.
Nous reconnaissons l'appui financier du gouvernement du Canada.

Weather Permitting
& Other Stories

Pratap Reddy

GUERNICA
EDITIONS
TORONTO • BUFFALO • LANCASTER (U.K.)
2016

Michael Mirolla, general editor
Sam Brown, editor
David Moratto, cover and interior design
Guernica Editions Inc.
1569 Heritage Way, Oakville, (ON), Canada L6M 2Z7
2250 Military Road, Tonawanda, N.Y. 14150-6000 U.S.A.
www.guernicaeditions.com

Distributors:
University of Toronto Press Distribution,
5201 Dufferin Street, Toronto (ON), Canada M3H 5T8
Gazelle Book Services, White Cross Mills, High Town,
Lancaster LA1 4XS U.K.

First edition.
Printed in Canada.

Legal Deposit – First Quarter
Library of Congress Catalog Card Number: 2015952391
Library and Archives Canada Cataloguing in Publication

"Reddy, Pratap, author
Weather permitting & other stories / Pratap Reddy. -- 1st edition.
(Essential prose series ; 122)
Short stories.
Issued in print and electronic formats.
ISBN 978-1-77183-056-0 (paperback).--ISBN 978-1-77183-057-7
(epub).-- ISBN 978-1-77183-058-4 (mobi)
1. Title. 11. Title: Weather permitting and other stories. 111. Series:
Essential prose series ; 122
PS8635.E337W43 2016   C813'.6   C2015-906645-X   C2015-906646-8

For my wife Shashi and my son Raj

Contents

Her White Christmas *1*

The Toy Flamingo *17*

Birthday Blues *33*

Ramki and the Christmas Trees *45*

Demon Glass *61*

Going West *73*

Weather Permitting *93*

The Tamarind Relish *121*

Mango Fool *133*

In the Dark *145*

That Which is Written *159*

For A Place in the Sun *173*

ACKNOWLEDGEMENTS *197*

ABOUT THE AUTHOR *199*

Her White Christmas

Wearing a thin, hand-knitted cardigan over her crumpled sari, Prema Sudhakar looks all of her sixty-odd years. It's late in the evening as she anxiously scans the collage of unfamiliar faces besieging her in the foyer of Pearson airport.

A young south Asian male enters the terminal but, noting his beard, her glance slides past him. The stranger walks right up to her.

"Hi, Mom," he says.

"Shyam! I didn't recognise you!"

Relief floods over Prema, moistening her eyes.

"Have you been waiting long, Mom?"

"No, only a few minutes. Yet, why are you late?"

"There was a traffic jam," Shyam says glibly.

"I was hoping you'd have changed after moving to Canada. Where's Shilpa?"

"She's at work."

"In her condition, she shouldn't be going to work, Shyam."

"Mom, things are different in Canada."

Shyam takes charge of the luggage and they proceed to the parking lot. Out in the open, Prema shivers.

"You'll need warmer clothes, Mom. Snow is expected next week."

"Do you think I'll get to see a white Christmas?"

"I'm sure you'll have your wish. The two winters I've seen were pretty bad."

"Will I be able to see the Aurora Borealis, too?"

"Aurora who?"

"Idiot! To think that your mother was a Geography teacher!"

Prema, like many educated Indians, had grown up reading books written almost exclusively by British and American authors. Travelling overseas is a dream-come-true opportunity to see firsthand what she had enjoyed in an armchair.

"By the way, how's my sister Apu?" Shyam asks.

Apu lives with her husband in an Austrian town with an unpronounceable name but a picturesque river front. They were both artists and had a habit of washing up in the unlikeliest of places.

"Shyam, it's you who ought to be telling me how Apu is. She lives abroad like you."

"Maybe, Mom, but Europe is pretty far from Canada. At the moment, we can't afford to visit her."

Haze hangs like a giant's breath over the city. Prema feels they have been driving forever, tailing a never-ending procession of red lights. The car slows as they turn on the street where Shyam lives. In the thickening dusk all the houses look alike in their drabness, pinpricks of light oozing out from within.

Shyam stops the car and steps out to open the car-door for his mother.

"Welcome to Canada, Mom!"

Prema trembles as a gust of polar wind washes over. She follows her son, her shoes crunching over fallen leaves. They enter a narrow row-house, one of many pressed together like slices in a loaf. Inside, an enormous staircase fills the hallway.

Prema sits down on a stool, and unbuckles her shoes.

"Mom, you relax in the living room while I fetch your suitcases."

Prema chooses to potter around the house: a few spartan and mismatched pieces of furniture—procured exclusively from garage-sales—are deployed here and there. On the kitchen countertop there are a pile of flyers and two unopened envelopes addressed to a Jojo Mbele.

The glass front-door closes with a slam. Shyam comes in, lugging two enormous suitcases.

"Mom, would you like dinner?"

"I'm full," she says, pulling a face. "I had something called Asian vegetarian meal on the plane."

Shyam unearths a packet of frozen rotis and a dish of leftover curry from the fridge. While he's heating them, Prema, who has already nosed around the kitchen, sets the table.

When he finishes his dinner, Shyam roots out a card from a kitchen drawer.

"Let's call Dad," he says.

Shyam fetches a cordless from the living room. Peering at the telephone card, he dials, disconnects, and dials again. He does this repeatedly while Prema regards him like an implacable deity.

"We use a card to call India. It's much cheaper."

"I'm not surprised," Prema says.

"It's ringing! Hi, Dad! I'm good. How are you? ... Mom, talk to Dad."

"Hello! I'm fine ... I guess she must be OK, she has gone to work ... yeah, you've heard it right. Is the maid coming to work every day ... I know it's only a day since I left India ... Goodnight ... Yes, it's night here ... Goodbye!"

Shyam takes the receiver from his mother, and both of them move out of the kitchen. They pause in the hallway, as though waiting for the next move in the gambit. Shyam is tired and wants to rest, while jetlag has made his mother disoriented and restless.

"Mom, you must be exhausted. May I show you to your room? It's on the second floor."

"I'll wait for Shilpa."

"It will be midnight when she returns."

"I don't mind. How does she come back?"

"I pick her up from the factory."

"No wonder you look so thin and tired. By the way, the beard doesn't suit you."

"I knew you'd say that, Mom. I'd like to go to my room now. I've had a long day."

"Suit yourself. I'll watch TV until Shilpa ..."

Prema stops short and her eyes widen. A young black male has just emerged from the staircase that leads to the basement. Dressed in a T shirt and shorts, he smiles at them.

"Did I startle you?" the man says.

"Mom, this is Joe, our tenant."

Prema somehow manages to find her tongue.

"Pleased to meet you," she says.

"Same, here. Sorry to intrude, but I won't take more than a minute."

"Take your time," Shyam says. "No hurry."

When Joe goes into the kitchen, Shyam and Prema step into the living room. Prema collapses into the nearest sofa, looking shell-shocked.

"Joe was renting the basement room when we bought the place. He came with the territory, so to speak."

"I don't know what to say."

"Mom, we need every penny we can lay our hands on. You've no idea of the mortgage payments ..."

"Shyam, I'm unable to understand how you could give a perfect stranger such ... free run of your home!"

"Joe's a very nice guy. He only comes up once or twice a day to do his cooking or use the toilet."

Prema shoots up like a rocket from the sofa.

"Please stop! I think I'll go to my room."

* * *

The next morning when Prema wakes, a pallid sun pretends to shine outside. The silence in the house is almost sepulchral: no birdsongs, no traffic sounds, nothing. Still groggy with jetlag, Prema forces herself to get up and go downstairs. She finds nobody about: it's as if the house is standing stock-still, holding its breath.

Prema makes herself a cup of coffee. Unable to find a newspaper, she goes through a stack of flyers. Later she tries to switch on the TV, but the universal remote proves too much of a challenge. She returns to the kitchen and cooks a south Indian breakfast, enjoying the explorer-like thrill of looking for, and finding, various vessels and ingredients.

At around noon, Shilpa comes out of her bedroom. She's wearing a kind of long loose T-shirt and seemingly little else.

"Shilpa! How nice to see you!"

Prema walks up to Shilpa and puts her arms around her.

"How are you feeling, my child?"

"Good, thank you."

She sounds formal, even standoffish.

"Are you taking good care of yourself?" Prema asks.

"Yes. Amma, I'm sorry, I didn't get to see you yesterday. You'd gone to bed when I came back."

"Never mind, dear. Would you like to have some *upma*?"

"Did you make it? How quickly you've learned to find your way around the house!"

The latter statement almost sounds like a rebuke. Ignoring it, Prema talks about the day Shyam was born. Shilpa remains mostly silent as she mechanically devours the breakfast.

"It was in the middle of the night and we went in a rickshaw to the hospital. Can you believe that?"

"Amma, I'm sorry, but I'll have to go and get ready now."

"It's OK, my dear. How do you go to work?"

"My supervisor picks me up."

"Oh," Prema says.

Shilpa returns, wearing an ill-fitting top and a crumpled pair of trousers.

"Everyone at the factory dresses like this," she says.

She gets into a scuffed pair of work-boots, and yanks out a genderless coat from the closet.

"Don't wait for me, Amma. Have your dinner with Shyam."

Prema peeps through the front window. She sees a dusty red pick-up drawn up on the road. Before climbing into the vehicle, Shilpa turns and looks at the window.

Prema steps back, as if stung.

* * *

Soon Prema takes complete charge of the house. Quickly learning the intricacies of the clothes-dryer, dishwasher and vacuum-cleaner, she sets about cleaning the house with the earnestness of an exorcist trying to dislodge demons.

One afternoon, after a frenetic bout of cleaning, she digs out a couple of incense sticks from her suitcase and lights them in the drawing room. Lazy curlicues of smoke rise, spreading the fragrance of sandalwood. Then all hell breaks loose.

A smoke-detector in the hallway begins to tweet, and then another joins in, creating an infernal cacophony. Prema stands paralyzed, her mind numb. Then she hears heavy footsteps racing up from the basement.

"What's happening?" Joe says.

He throws the offending joss-sticks into the kitchen sink and turns on the exhaust. The smoke-detectors fall silent, and Prema feels a rush of affection for Joe.

"Thank you so much. I just didn't know what to do."

"Lady, if you really want to play with fireworks, do it in the park down the road, OK?"

Taking the flight of steep steps that leads out of the hallway, Joe disappears into his netherworld.

Prema is unable to get back into the swing of things. She puts her cleaning frenzy on hold, turns on the TV, and settles down in front of it with seeming contentment, though the shows are of little interest to her. When Shyam returns from work, Prema recounts her escapade.

"Where did you find a matchbox to light those damn things?"

"I've been on the lookout ever since I came. Yesterday, when I was dusting the furniture I found a cigarette-lighter wedged in the side of the loveseat. Shyam, I hope you haven't ..."

"Mom, please don't jump to conclusions. No, I have not started smoking again. Shilpa doesn't smoke either. Funny, how the lighter got in there."

"Well, if you buy used furniture, what else can you expect? By the way, Shyam, I've been looking for an electric iron, too. I'd like to wear pressed clothes even if you and Shilpa don't care to."

"Point taken. We'll buy one today. Anyways, it's time I got you some winter clothes."

Later, they drive down to a nearby mall. The trees along the way are bare; yellow and orange pools have collected on the ground as if the trees have sprung a leak.

"Is everything OK between you and Shilpa?"

"Why do you ask? Of course everything is OK!"

"Things don't seem the same. Shilpa has become so ... so remote."

"Mom, it's your imagination. Life can be very stressful for immigrants. Besides, even when we were living in India, you never quite liked Shilpa just because she comes from a different province."

"You know that's nonsense," Prema says.

"Once you make up your mind, Mom, it's hard to convince you otherwise."

"Shyam, you've begun to talk like your father."

At the store, they pick up a coat, gloves and snow-boots, all from a section marked 'Clearance'. Unable to find an iron there, Shyam wheels the cart to the aisle which carries small appliances. To his mother's wonderment, he homes in unerringly on the cheapest one.

* * *

A few days later, it snows for the first time. It starts off gently like a shower of jasmine petals but soon turns into an uproarious maelstrom. Prema, who's all alone in the house, shuffles timorously to the window to take a peek: the entire neighbourhood is being submerged in drifts of fleece.

In the afternoon, the sky clears as if by magic and sunlight spills like molten gold on to the landscape. Prema puts on her winter gear and ventures out into the yard. Her legs sink almost knee-deep in the snow. She pulls out her gloves and scoops up handfuls of snow to make a snowball. Feeling shy all of a sudden she tosses the ball away and returns indoors—happy as a child.

In the days that follow there are a few flurries and some rain—but hardly any snow. Prema has a sneaking feeling that she'll never get to see a white Christmas.

One afternoon, when Prema is single-mindedly pressing clothes, the door bell rings. Setting the iron down on its rump, she goes to open the door. There's a young white male standing at the doorstep. Prema sees a red pick-up idling in the driveway.

"I've come for Shilpa," he says.

He's unshaven and reeks of nicotine. His eyes are cobalt blue.

"She should've been ready by now. Let me go up and see."

Upstairs, Shilpa's fast asleep. Prema doesn't have the heart to wake her. She creeps back downstairs.

"Shilpa's resting. She will not be able to come to work."

"I wish she had called and saved me the trouble of driving down."

"I'm sorry about that. She's fast asleep; she couldn't have possibly called you."

The young man shrugs and leaves, looking peeved. The truck backs out with a roar and races away.

Prema returns to her ironing, but she's disturbed and doesn't know why she feels so. However much she presses, she's unable to flatten out some of the wrinkles.

When Shilpa emerges from her room in the afternoon, she's cross.

"I wish you had wakened me," she says.

"Shilpa, this is your first pregnancy. You must be careful, child."

"I know. But I don't like losing a day's pay."

"Why? Don't you have sick leave, or something?"

"No work, no pay. It's as simple as that."

When Shyam returns from work, he's drawn into the debate even before he can kick off his boots.

"Shilpa, it's time you stopped going to work," he says.

"It's you who insisted I take up a job."

"Yeah, we've a big mortgage to pay off. You wouldn't listen when I said this place was too big for us."

"Yes, everything is my fault. It wasn't my idea to come to Canada in the first place."

The conversation graduates from a mild disagreement to an argument, threatening to grow into something larger. Prema, who always had difficulty in maintaining order in a classroom, feels utterly ineffectual.

"Shyam, this isn't the time to argue," Prema says at last. "Shilpa's health is the first priority."

Shilpa unexpectedly begins to sob, and Shyam rushes to console her. Prema retires to the kitchen under the pretext of making some strong south Indian coffee, her remedy for calming inflamed nerves. Prema has never witnessed a quarrel between Shyam and Shilpa before and her suspicion that not everything is hunky-dory between them grows stronger.

Shilpa was not her choice for a daughter-in-law. Shyam in his purblind way, as usual, had fallen in love, and forestalled her search for a suitable girl. All said and done Prema like any mother desperately wants her son's marriage to be happy and successful.

* * *

On the night before Christmas, Prema looks out of her window: there are coloured lights hanging outside some houses. A few stubborn daubs of ice remain on the rooftops but the street is bereft of snow. A bedraggled patch of grass is plainly visible under the street lamps.

"Well, it's going to be a green Christmas," she says to herself as she gets into her bed.

Prema has a dream: It is Shyam's wedding. Shilpa makes an entrance wearing a red bridal sari, while the band plays a traditional tune. The very next moment, Shilpa is seen in jeans and a T-shirt. Outraged, Prema turns to look at Shyam. But the man seated in front of the sacred fire is not Shyam but Joe. The musicians beat loudly on the drums.

Prema is jolted out of her dream; there's someone knocking on her door.

"Mom, I think Shilpa's in labour. I'll have to take her to the hospital."

"Do you want me to come with you?" Prema asks, opening the door.

"No, Mom. It may take a long time, and you may have to wait endlessly in the visitor's area. You hold the fort while we're gone. If we need anything, I'll call you."

Carrying an infant car seat, and a small duffel bag packed with Shilpa's belongings, Shyam and Shilpa leave for the hospital.

Prema goes back to bed, but sleep eludes her. She makes herself a cup of coffee, and watches TV with indifference. She dozes off and then shakes herself awake, she does this repeatedly.

At around 10 am the phone rings.

"Mom, it's a boy!" Shyam says.

"I'm so happy for you!"

Later, Shyam takes Prema to the hospital to see the newborn. The baby is in a bassinet beside Shilpa's bed. Shilpa looks pale and tired.

"How are you feeling, my child?" says Prema.

"I'm fine."

Prema picks up the child, uttering sweet nothings in Telugu.

The baby is pink and roly-poly, with brown, downy hair. Even as she's cradling him in her arms, the baby opens his eyes for a fleeting moment. A pair of blue eyes stares back at Prema.

Prema hands over the baby to Shilpa, as if they are playing hot potatoes.

"Anything wrong, Mom?" asks Shyam.

Prema looks at Shilpa. But her daughter-in-law's face is turned away. They sit for some time in awkward silence. A puzzled Shyam offers to take Prema home.

On the way back, Shyam puts on the radio. A babbling DJ offers to play one of Irving Berlin's best pieces.

"Please switch off the radio!" Prema says.

"Why, it's the *White Christmas*! Don't you want to listen to it?"

"No! You must make the reservation for me to return to India."

"You can't go back now, Mom!"

"Please do as I say."

"Has something happened? Are you annoyed with us for some reason?"

"It has nothing to do with you. I just feel like going back home, and don't argue with me."

"I'm disappointed that you are leaving. Shilpa will be upset, I'm sure."

Shyam thinks he hears his mother emit a snort.

"Mom, you always wanted to visit Apu. Would you rather I booked a ticket to Austria?"

"That can wait. I want to go back home now. If you don't want to get my return journey confirmed, let me know. I can do it on my own."

Unannounced, it starts to snow. It falls like salt and bounces off the windscreen. The flurries grow thicker and the road looks paved with stardust. When Shyam brings the car to a halt on their driveway, Prema steps out. The fresh snow crackles underfoot.

"Mom, you've got to see a white Christmas after all."

"You bet," says Prema, with an emphasis that surprises Shyam.

* * *

A few days after his mother's return to India, Shyam's father calls him.

"Dad, please hang up the phone," Shyam says. "I'll call you back."

"Don't bother, Shyam. I've heard of your notorious phone cards. Nowadays international calls have become quite cheap in India too."

"Dad, how is Mom? She became very upset when she was here. I don't know why. I asked her what was wrong many times, but as usual she didn't bother to explain."

"She's fine, believe me. Your mother has gone to the club for a game of rummy. About her becoming upset—that's the reason why I'm calling you. Shyam, don't take this to heart—she has got it into her head that the child is not yours."

"That's sheer nonsense!"

"You're right. But your mother bases her suspicion on the colour of the baby's eyes," his father says.

"I can't believe it! Dad, you've met Shilpa's relatives—they're from the west coast, and quite a few of them have light-coloured eyes."

"I know, Shyam. That's what I've been trying to tell your mother. Shyam, you shouldn't feel bad—you know about your mother, don't you? She can be difficult at times."

There's the wisdom of a long-suffering life in Shyam's father's voice. Shyam is silent for a few moments. Though he ought to have been inured to his mother's opinionated views, he wishes things were different.

"Shyam, are you there?"

"Yes, Dad, very much. Is Mom still annoyed with us?"

"No. She seems to have gotten over it apparently. She's planning a trip to Austria."

"That's good to hear. I'm sure Apu will be able to keep her happy."

His father chuckles. "I won't bet on it, Shyam. Your mother wants to see the blue Danube. For Apu's sake, I hope the river lives up to its reputation."

The Toy Flamingo

itting squished on a single leather chair, my two young daughters looked like Siamese twins as they leafed through a big picture book they had on their laps. Dressed alike in a pink and white outfit with matching co-ordinates—my wife Anita was finicky in such matters, they looked so young and innocent.

"Hi sweethearts," I said, dropping my car keys and cell phone into a walnut-wood tray we had bought in India while on holiday. It was a Sunday afternoon, and I had just returned from a meeting organized by a nature conservation society in Mississauga.

"*Da*-ddy!" both of them exclaimed. Extricating themselves from the chair, Veena, aged 6, placed the book on a side table, while Neena, all of 5, shuffled towards me, weighed down by the gift-wrapped parcel in her hands. They shouted: "Look, what we've got for you!"

"Children, wish your Daddy a Happy Father's Day!" said Mummy-ji, my wife Anita's mother, emerging from the kitchen where she must have been having a cup of chai while her daughter cooked dinner. Since Anita called her mother 'Mummy', I would add the honorific 'ji' while addressing her. After my father-in-law's death about a year ago, Mummy-ji, who lived all by herself in Brampton, began to drop by more often than I cared. While I was passionate about nature, and wanted to lead a life which was in harmony with our environment, Mummy-ji, it appeared to me, admired success, and the power it gave you to acquire status symbols. I would hate it if Anita and the children came under her influence.

"I think it is such an important day," she added pointedly. It was my mother-in-law's perennial plaint that I never observed the red-letter days in one's life—Father's Day, Valentine's Day etc.—with the fervour they deserved. Knowing full well that nothing special would be done on this notable occasion (for Anita, understandably, would be keen only on Mother's day), she had purposefully driven down and taken the girls to a nearby mall to buy their Daddy a present.

"I agree, Mummy-ji," I said, giving my daughters a hug and a kiss each.

"Sunita's husband Ajay would always give his children return gifts on Father's day," said Mummy-ji.

I ignored her comment. Sunita was Mummy-ji's elder daughter, who along with her family had relocated to Australia a couple of years ago, citing Canada's extreme weather as a pretext. In that insular continent they were happily impervious to Mummy-ji's weekly visits.

The gift I received, going by its size and heft, seemed to be a book. Though it was more than a decade since I came to Canada, I hadn't quite overcome the Indian custom of *not* opening gifts the moment one received them.

Anita entered the room and headed straight for the TV remote. My wife bore a strong resemblance to her mother and had the same nervous energy in her movements.

"What did the children give you, Venky?" she asked, pointing the remote like a dagger at the TV.

"A book, I'm guessing," I said, starting to tear open the package.

The TV screen—the size of a small billboard, no less—crackled and came to life. The children stopped reading, and turned their heads to watch an ecstatic woman talking about the increased whitening power of an age-old brand of toothpaste.

The book I unwrapped was called *Winged Visitors*. The gift brought a smile to my lips: even my young children were aware of my keen interest in nature. Left to her, Mummy-ji would have bought me a book on how to become a millionaire in seven days. Maybe I was being unduly harsh, but when Mummy-ji was around I felt like a wild bird which has been thrust into a cage.

On the front cover of the book my girls gave me, a host of flamingos stood rooted in knee-deep water. But my mind was not on the book, it was drawn elsewhere:

I see the rose-pink bird through a mist of tears. It is made from a stiff sheet of paper, and is mounted on a stick. The bird has an S-shaped neck and a big beak. Crude, black strokes outline its body.

I wipe my eyes and raise my hand to grab the bird. He pulls the toy out of my reach. His unshaven cheeks look as if has rubbed soot on them.

He shows me how the toy works. When he pushes

up a slider on the stick, the bird lifts it wings. And when
he brings the slider down, the bird lowers its wings.

Taking the toy from him, I move the slider up and
down, again and again: the bird flaps its wings as if
it's flying through the air.

"A penny for your thoughts," Anita said.

"It's nothing," I said. I had been plagued by such unbidden thoughts as far back as I could remember. When I was very young, they would occur often, popping up at unexpected moments, but as I grew older they had become less frequent. The funny thing was that the people who appeared in them were certainly not my parents; I would always be very young and speak in a tongue which was gibberish to me. The events bore no obvious relationship to my life as I knew it. Yet the memories must have had some connection with my childhood which I couldn't figure out. Whatever the reason, when I did experience them, they caused an indescribable sadness within me ...

* * *

The next week, on a Friday night, we stood holding the free drinks we had exchanged for the tickets handed to us at the door. Except for the lighted stage where a group of dancers were gyrating to Bollywood songs, the place was in semi-darkness. Waves of guests surged and swirled around us, talking, laughing, drinking, eating.

I cannot remember now whether it was a party to launch a South Asian Magazine, or an East Indian fashion show; Anita worked in an ad agency, so she was always being called out. To please Anita, I would accompany her and stand by her elbow, ready to fetch up a smile whenever someone approached us. Sometimes, I was too quick on the draw and ended up shaking hands with perfect strangers, much to Anita's annoyance.

A buffet was arranged at the far end of the room. We joined a line up which made a halting progress towards the spread, the cynosure of the party. In the only light that came from the chafing dishes, the food looked like nothing recognizable. But I need not have worried; they were mostly South Asian stuff like nans, tandoori chicken and potato tikkis masquerading as western fare.

In the semidarkness, while biting into the tidbits, uninvited a memory entered my consciousness:

He is in the kitchen—I can hear the banging of vessels. I'm hungry; I've been sitting at the table for ages.

"Hasve agataday!" I cry out. The room is small and dingy, illuminated with a bulb of low wattage hanging from a wire.

Something falls to the ground with a crash. I hear him mutter in a strange language. I'm certain now that dinner will take even longer to come.

We left the party at eleven, and drove to Mummy-ji's place. Whenever we go out, we leave our children in her care, like a couple of bags in a left-luggage office.

"I don't like it Anita ..." I said.

"I know the party was a bore. I'm sorry."

"No, it's not the party. We leave the children to themselves much too often."

"Come on, we are leaving them with my mother. And it's not as if we are leaving them with a baby-sitter. We are not paying my mother anything, you know."

"It's not about money. It's just that the girls need to get a good night's sleep."

"You don't expect me to stay back at home every evening and take care of them, do you!"

"I don't. But we are doing it too often."

"Venky, this is only the third time this week we have been out!"

I parked the car in the driveway, behind Mummy-ji's Buick. Mummy-ji lived in a rambling house with a large backyard, for which my father-in-law was paying a hefty mortgage right until he died. She was always goading Anita to graduate to at least a semi from the small, but adequate, townhouse we were living in. Often Mummy-ji reminded me that Sunita and Ajay had lived in a detached house before they left Canada.

"Did you have a nice time?" asked Mummy-ji, as she opened the door.

"Guess what, I met Pooja Sharma at the party ..." Anita began to say.

"I'll get the girls," I said and went up to the guest bedroom. They were sleeping in the fashion children do—bodies askew and limbs all higgledy-piggledy. I picked up Veena and returned to the drawing room.

"The samosas were good, but the dip just didn't go with them," Anita was saying. My wife tore herself away from her conversation and went up to fetch Neena, living up to her strongly held belief that we should share all our duties in equal portion. I grew up in a house where mom and dad had different sets of duties—very old fashioned no doubt.

Meanwhile, though it was almost midnight, Mummy-ji felt obliged to engage me with small talk.

"How are your parents?" she asked.

"They're doing fine."

My parents lived in Kingston; my dad worked as a teaching assistant in a nearby university. He had put in more than a decade's service as a professor in India, and after moving to Canada he had somehow managed to land a job associated with teaching. It was a miracle that he had not ended up as a cab-driver like so many highly qualified immigrants. My mother had been a housewife most of her life. But in Canada she had to go to work—doing a series of part time jobs at fast food joints, coin laundries and garment shops—to make ends meet. Now, after having paid off the mortgage, she was content to stay at home and take care of her husband, house, and garden.

"The next time you meet your mother, remind her about the recipe for sambaar," Mummy-ji said.

Anita came down clutching Neena to her bosom. Outside, the night was thrumming with the call of crickets. An owl hooted in the woods behind the house. In the eerie light that filtered down through the trees, we carried our sleeping children to the car.

She's sleeping in the middle of the drawing room. Why doesn't she get up and give me something to eat? She's lying on a cot, wearing all those flowers. She doesn't move, not even when all those people go around her,

with their hands folded in prayer. I'm feeling hungry.
The man with unshaven face has told me to wait as he
was busy. He is standing in a corner, whispering to
the stream of people who come up to him and hold
his hand.

I drove the car in silence.

"Why are you so quiet?" Anita asked. "Is anything wrong?"

"No. It's just that I keep remembering things from my childhood."

"What things?"

"I know it sounds stupid, but things that are not part of my conscious memory. I mean, I don't recollect having met these people. And the peculiar thing is, my parents are never around."

"When did it start? You've said nothing about it to me."

"They started ages ago, right from when I was little boy. But the frequency began to reduce as I was growing up. Now they have started appearing again."

"What could be the reason for them, I wonder?"

"I'm not sure." I forbore to say that the increased frequency pretty much coincided with Mummy-ji's new found interest—interference, really—in our lives. "But whatever the reason, they always make me feel sad. Unbearably sad."

"Could they be something to do with your previous life?" Anita asked, with doubt in her voice. Being Hindus, the idea of reincarnation came too easily to our minds.

"I doubt it. There must be a more prosaic explanation. I'd have called them memories but for the fact that they don't seem to have any relation to my life."

"Have you spoken to your parents about it?"

"No, never. These dreams or visions or whatever—they were like some very private grief, they were not nightmares or anything, so it never occurred to me to share it with my parents. You are right, perhaps, I should talk to my parents about it. I'll go to Kingston tomorrow."

"I thought you wanted to take the girls for a trek in the woods along the Credit River?"

"I'll have to put it off to the next weekend, however much I was keen to take them. It has been a long time since I've seen my parents, anyway. Poor Dad. I didn't give him so much as a phone call on Father's Day!"

* * *

On Saturday afternoon, after finishing all the jobs Anita had earmarked for me—empty and clean the vacuum cleaner, get grocery from both local and Indian stores, bring the children back from their weekly piano lesson—I drove alone to Kingston.

The house stood on the last lot of a crescent. A pear tree brooded over a lawn no bigger than an area rug. A pair of robins hopped about in the shade of the tree, poking their noses in the grass.

I parked the car on the bare driveway. My dad's car was always stowed in the garage, but at our house in Mississauga, out-of-order appliances, out-of-fashion clothes, and out-of-favour toys had nudged the two cars out of the garage.

My dad opened the door even before I could ring the bell. He was wearing a golf shirt and a pair of sweat pants.

My dad turned his head and announced loudly, as if I were a train or something: "Venkat has arrived!"

My mom bustled into the room from the kitchen, holding a spatula in her hand. She was wearing a crumpled sari; after moving to Canada, my mom had given up the habit of wearing pressed clothes every day as too much of an indulgence.

"You've lost a lot of weight," she said.

"Mom, I've put on ten pounds. As matter of fact, I'm thinking of joining a gym."

Even before I could get out of my shoes and take a seat, she rushed back into the kitchen as though the apparent loss in my weight demanded immediate remediation. There was no dearth of food ever in my parents' home, and Anita, like her family, gave a lot of importance to rich food, yet I couldn't help wondering as to why I am haunted by memories of going hungry.

The house was cool and tidy, and smelled faintly of the spices my mom used in the kitchen. The rooms were furnished with do-it-yourself stuff from Ikea and Wal-Mart. Near a window, a wrought iron cage, empty and forlorn, hung from the ceiling; once upon a time, I had kept a pair of peachface lovebirds in it.

"How are Anita and the children?" my dad asked.

"Fine," I said. To all the queries my parents threw at me in Telugu, I always replied in English.

My mom served me a masala dosa, a rice crepe folded over a filling of sautéed potatoes. Tearing off rag-like bits of the dosa, I dipped them in chutney and ate them.

"Dad, what does *hasve agataday* mean?" I said. "Is it Tamil?"

"No, it is Kannada," my dad said. "It means, 'I'm feeling hungry.' But why do you ask?"

"I remember using those words long ago. I also remember being often hungry. There was a man—I can recall his face but not his name or anything."

My dad remained silent.

I laughed and added: "Anita thinks it is something from my previous life!"

"If I were you, I wouldn't bother too much about it. How's your work? No layoffs in your company I hope? I hear there's lot of downsizing going on everywhere."

" Dad, about the visions I have ..."

"Your plate is empty. You should have another dosa ... Radha! A dosa for Venkat, please."

"Give me a minute," my mother shouted back from the kitchen.

"Dad, about the man I remember seeing long ago," I persisted, despite my dad trying to sidetrack my questions. "I remember him so clearly. He had stubble on his chin. It would prickle me whenever he kissed me on my cheek."

"Is it only now that you have begun to think of him?" my dad said.

"No, I used to think of him a lot when I was a kid. Sometimes, he would appear in my dreams. But over the years, it had become less frequent. But of late I have been thinking of him again."

"Did anything in happen in your life to occasion the return of these memories?"

"Nothing I know of."

"Is everything OK at home?"

"Pretty much," I said, choosing not to disclose how

stifling it was to live with Mummy-ji's shadow hanging constantly over us.

"Are you sure?"

"Of course, Dad! Coming back to what I was saying —when I was reminded of that man again the other day, I felt I should speak to you. Maybe you would know something about him."

There was no response from my dad. My little speech seemed to have sucked all the sounds out of the room.

"Well," my dad said, after a few minutes, running his tongue over his lower lip. "I don't know where to begin ..."

My mom, who had entered the room, was holding a dosa balanced on a large spatula. Having heard what I had said, she demanded: "Who has been telling you all these things?"

"Nobody," I said. "It's just that I remember some incidents ..."

"Where's the need to dig up the past?" she said. "Nothing good is going to come out of it."

"Radha, he is grown up now. It is our duty to tell him, whether we like it or not. Venkat, I wanted to talk to you about it when you turned twenty-one. But your mother dissuaded me."

"I don't see any point in his knowing," my mother said.

"Knowing what?" I said.

"Well Venkat, it might come as shock to you. You are ... you are not our biological son."

"Dad, what are you saying?"

"How does it matter?" my mom cut in, dropping the dosa on my plate. "You are my sister's son, which is just as good."

"Your father appeared out of the blue one day and asked us to care of you," my dad said.

"Like how your colleague Dr. Peters gave me the caged cockatoo to take care of when he was going away to Germany?" I said.

"Don't be ridiculous," my dad said. "Your father didn't have the means to look after you. There were days, I believe, when you both didn't have a morsel to eat. What your father did was in your best interest."

"You were barely four when you came to our house," my mom said. "You looked so thin and small. You sat on the edge of a chair, clutching a toy bird. It looked like a crane or something."

"It was a flamingo," I said absently.

My dad smiled, for no apparent reason it seemed.

"If you really want to know," my mom said, "my sister Jaya had married Mahesh—that's your father—against our parents' wishes. Mahesh was from a different caste and spoke a different language. Jaya was the youngest child and our father's favourite. When he didn't give his consent, she simply walked out. Taking nothing but the clothes she stood in. She was a very proud girl. That was the last we saw of her. The day your father brought you to our house, we came to know that Jaya was no more. You might not remember her ..."

"I do, mom," I said. "I have a memory of the day she died."

Silence came stomping back into the room. After what seemed like hours, my mom said, in a voice strained by unshed tears: "My poor boy."

"What about my father? Is he still alive?" I asked.

"No, he died two years later," my dad said. "They both died of tuberculosis. Back home, the treatment is very expensive. From what I heard, your father never had a regular job. It must have been very hard for them."

"What did he do for a living?"

"He never had a steady job because ..."

"In India, who will give a job to—what's the word for a person who studies birds?" my mom said.

"An ornithologist?" I said.

"That's right," my mom said. "Every time you asked for a pet parakeet or a cockatoo, my heart would get a jolt. It was relief when you graduated from university and got yourself a real job."

"We are sorry, Venkat. We had decided not to tell you about your past, perhaps it was a mistake."

"Dad, I'm sure you had my best interests at heart."

"Both your parents were dead," my mom said. "So what was the purpose of telling you about them? It was not like we were keeping you away from them."

"Actually, Venkat, even your real father—"

"Dad," I said, "you are my real father."

My dad smiled. "Thank you, son. Well, your biological father wanted it kept that way. Maybe, that's the reason why he didn't show himself again."

"I saw him a couple of times, though," I said.

"What do you mean?" my mother said.

"Do you remember the old house in Hyderabad? I used to spend most of my afternoons looking out of the playroom window on the second floor. He would walk by the house, on the opposite side of the lane, throwing a glance or two at the house."

"What a funny thing to do," my mom said. "He could have stepped in for a few minutes ..."

"Radha," my dad said.

"I'd wave out to him, but he never saw me," I said.

"Unfortunately, Venkat, your father was one of those people who couldn't do anything right," my mom said. "The only wise thing he did in his life was to bring you to us." After a pause she said, as if adding a postscript: "May his soul rest in peace."

That was that: my mom didn't want to dwell too much on the topic. It was obvious that my mom held my biological father responsible for what had happened to her sister. I didn't want to probe too much either, lest I hurt my parents—the people who parented me, pampered me, loved me—by showing too much eagerness.

Later, when it was time for me to return, my parents came to the car to see me off. My mom gave me a small box packed with Mysore pak, a south Indian sweet she had made for Anita and the children. Even though my head was abuzz with so many thoughts, I couldn't help wondering how peculiar it was that Indian sweets were so often named after towns: Mysore pak, Bombay halwa, Agra petha, Bandar laddu.

It was almost nine, but the sun had not yet turned in for the night. The trees in the street were alive with the chirping of sparrows. A ring-billed gull moved across the sky, lazily flapping its wings.

"Venkat, your father didn't do much for you in his life," my dad said. "But he bequeathed his love of nature to you."

"I'll remember that, Dad."

While I had to cope with the problem of Mummy-ji by

myself, I had also learned how enduring the legacy of parents' love and values could be. As I drove away, I turned my head and looked back. My mom and dad were standing there with their hands raised, staring after my car.

I look out of the window. I see people on the street. Now and then a rickshaw trundles by. Sometimes a car races past, its horn blaring.

Then I see him. He is walking down the lane, not so fast this time. When he draws level with the gate, he stops. He stands there with his hand on the latch, undecided. I wave out, but he does not see me.

He stares at the front door for a few moments and then raises his palm to his mouth, and in a gesture of affection, kisses his fingers. Abruptly he turns and walks away, without a backward glance.

I never see him again.

Birthday Blues

I woke up on the morning of my 12th birthday and immediately wished I hadn't. It was almost ten and the house had that deathly Sunday stillness. I went to the washroom, peed, wiped the seat clean of the yellow drops and flushed the toilet—all as mum had trained me to do.

I went back to my room and picked up *The Dark Knight Returns*. Lying down on my bed, I began to read. Reading kept my mind off things like how dorky *all* my birthdays had been. OK not all, at least the ones I could remember. I needed no crystal ball to tell me that the present one would be no different.

I heard a sudden *vroom* downstairs—mum must have started on her favourite weekend pastime, vacuuming the whole damn universe. It was only a matter of time before she came upstairs, dragging the machine like pit bull on a leash. I got up and played Back Street Boys (which mum had bought for me for no other reason than it had a red sticker) real loud to drown the racket she was making.

Soon enough, without so much as a knock, mum pushed my bedroom door open. Mum believed in surprising people.

"There's no *need* to put on the music that loud," she said.

I got up and tweaked the controls—pretending to reduce the volume. It had been an entirely different ball game when Joe was around.

Mum shut the door and I went back to my book. A couple of seconds later, she opened the door again.

"Happy Birthday, son. What would you like to do today?"

What I'd like to do? Go bowling with my buddies, Tony and Mustapha, that's what. But I kept the thought to myself. With mum within earshot, it was not very wise to air your thoughts.

"Shall we go to the temple?" she asked brightly. I wanted to groan. She continued: "First, I'll make some food for your dad."

Dad had died two years ago, exactly on the same date as my birthday. Mum would cook for him and place the food on a small table below his framed photograph on a wall in the living room. Later, we'd eat the leftovers—some birthday treat.

Don't get me wrong. Dad had been a good dude. I wouldn't say the same thing of Joe. Though dad could be cantankerous at times, he had been a chummy kind of person. If I did something stupid, he'd roll his eyes and say, *Je*-sus! He used to say that all the time even though he was a full-blown Hindu, born and bred in India.

Mum too was born in India. But you wouldn't have guessed, looking at her. She always wore stuff like tops and pants, and her hair was cut very short. Even her accent didn't sound Indian (neither did it sound very Canadian, though she would have dearly wanted it to).

Dad's parents had seen mum in a photograph a relative had sent them from India. In the picture, mum was wearing a sari, and she had flowers in her long hair and a big red dot on her forehead. According to mum, my grand-parents took such a shine to her that they boarded the next plane to India and arranged for dad's marriage.

After mum finally left my room, I got back to my book. I liked reading—I devoured graphic novels by the ton. When I grow up I'd like to be a writer. I like words—nice long words, words with a majestic ring to them. Unfortunately, my spelling sucked. Miss Bowman, my class teacher, said that you must know how to spell if you wanted to be a writer.

"No sweat," Tony said, "you can always use the spell check."

But Mustapha said: "Only ninnies use spell check."

* * *

On the evening of my tenth birthday, dad tried to string a bowtie around my neck. Unlike mum, dad was tall and heavily-built with large clumsy hands. He appeared a little out of breath and droplets of sweat formed on his brow as he struggled with the tie. It was August and the weather was hot and stuffy. Mum never switched the AC on until the temperature touched 100 degrees—Celsius, mind you, not Fahrenheit.

Mum had bought me a black pinstripe suit to wear to my birthday party at Chuckee Cheese. When dad said that nobody wore a suit to Chuckee Cheese, mum simply steam-rolled over his objections—like always.

Mum had invited all her friends, her relatives and *their*

children to the party. But Tony and Mustapha were nowhere in the guest list—you'd think it was Mum's birthday party.

"Can't you tie a bowtie properly?" mum said to dad.

She roughly spun me in her direction and started to manipulate the bowtie. I was half-afraid I'd get strangled to death.

"It's loose. You'll have to tighten it," dad said.

That darn tie was choking me as it was.

"So you think you know everything, eh?" mum said.

That's how it started. Before I could even get into my pinstripe coat, they were screaming at each other. Then came the usual Act Two where things got physical. Dad gave mum a slap on her shoulder. And mum replied in kind—with a sort of a punch in his stomach. I watched the bout mutely like a referee who had misplaced his whistle.

They stopped fighting just as suddenly and got on with the job of getting ready as if nothing had happened—like they always did. But as dad was about to pick up his car keys, he gave out a loud moan—as though somebody was tying a bowtie very tightly around his throat. He fell down with a crash, breaking a leg of an end table. Mum screamed and dialled 911.

We accompanied dad in the ambulance because mum didn't know how to drive. I sat in my pinstripe trousers and bowtie next to him. Mum was continually on the mobile, calling her friends and relatives to cancel the party. The paramedic heard her and wished me a "Happy Birthday." Dad looked at me, rolled his eyes and mouthed: "*Je*-sus!"

When we got out of the ambulance we found that some of my parents' friends and relatives had decided to follow us to the hospital. Perhaps, they wanted to give mum and dad moral support. Or did they think that the venue of the party had moved? Seeing the long line-up of cars—like a preview of his funeral procession—must have unnerved dad.

He never got out of the hospital alive. I miss dad. I think he had loved me in his own peculiar way, whatever mum said to the contrary.

* * *

It was a foregone conclusion that my 11th birthday would be a no go. After all it was dad's anniversary too. It kind of sucked he died on my birthday. But when such thoughts occurred to me I felt bad because it was like being disloyal to dad. I missed not having him around a helluva lot. Mum, who had been weepy for days, kept saying that she missed dad.

As a sparring partner, I thought. One way or another I couldn't see the two of us trying to restart the abandoned party in Chuckee Cheese.

Mum made chicken tikka and fried rice and offered them to dad. They were his favourite Indian dishes. At lunch time she removed the stone-cold food from below dad's picture and placed it on the dining table.

"The food tastes funny," I said. "I think it needs some salt."

"That's right," mum said. "Dr. Moore had told me to use less salt in the cooking because your dad was—what's the word?"

"Hypersensitive," I suggested.

"Whatever," mum said. "But I never got around to doing it when your dad was alive."

In the evening we went to a temple. We took the bus because we didn't own a car. Mum hadn't yet met Joe. The temple was in a quiet neighbourhood but it had no dome or spire or anything. It could have been mistaken for an office block—I mean, it didn't look like the Taj Mahal, or something grand like that.

Inside, a wine-red carpet stretched from wall to wall. On a raised platform, life-size statues of Hindu deities sat in a row looking straight ahead, as though waiting to be introduced to the gathering. Mum walked up to each one of them with both her palms joined together, whispering all the while. I trailed behind mum, doing a fair imitation of her actions hoping that I too would look religious.

In a corner, a half naked *pujari* sat on the floor distributing holy water and prasad. He spoke to us in Hindi. The priest looked newly arrived from India. A *jnaani*-come-lately, mum said. Mum thought she's got a great sense of humour. *That's* the real joke, let me tell you.

On our way back, mum stopped at Wal-Mart. She bought a crappy boombox which was on sale as a birthday present for me. There were guys in my class who got expensive gizmos on their birthdays. I wished mum had bought me something cool like a Play Station or a Gameboy. Something that would have made Tony and Mustapha's jaws drop.

* * *

Joginder was mum's instructor at *Singh Along Driving School for Ladies*. After helping her get a license, Joe took the liberty of renting our basement. "To lighten our burden," mum said. "Besides, it's good for you to have a father figure around."

There's no denying we were hard up. Mum was doing mostly temp jobs. Even when she had a good job, she was constantly poring over the help wanted columns in newspapers. That's because she couldn't get along with her bosses—she found them too bossy.

Though Joe had rented only the basement, he was upstairs most of the time. Wearing a tacky golf shirt and a pair of shorts, he would strut about the house showing off his hairy limbs. He would have a big bulge in his crotch as though he was carrying a pet turtle between his legs. A nice father figure he cut.

Very soon, Joe, in his boorish way, started invading mum's room. I would hear him beyond the wall, making jokes about his students and laughing his guts out. Instead of kicking him out, mum would join in sometimes. God, I could never understand adults. Whenever Joe was with mum, I turned on the boombox full blast. Throwing music like a coverlet over my head, I'd try to go to sleep.

Before long, even mum's patience with Joe began to wear thin. He was always tardy with his rent, and mum had discovered he was more of an expense than an asset. Besides, he never gave her any help around the house; repairing his car was all the work Joe did. Every weekend, he'd settle down on the driveway to fix his old Ford. Even then the jalopy always gave trouble. Often we'd find ourselves sitting in the car, marooned in the middle of a busy road as Joe tried to fix something or the other under the hood. Quietly seething, mum would try to play something on the car stereo, but she would find only CD's of *bhangra* music, and this would annoy her even more. If I had a doozy device like an MP3 player, I would play something civilized—and not the crummy Bollywood songs which mum liked. Mum, not being of the kind to give up easily, was constantly after Joe, wanting him to run errands for her. And Joe began to change —he'd disappear into his basement for long stretches and, whenever he emerged, he looked sullen and scrappy.

On Saturday morning, a day before my 12th birthday, I woke up late. I heard Joe's steam-bellow snores in the bedroom next-door. I got up and played music loud. It flushed him out of the room in a blink.

"Buddy, why do put on the music so loud?" Joe asked.

"I don't like the sounds you make in mum's room," I said. That set him on his way.

A little later I heard a commotion in the kitchen. Joe was getting an earful, louder than my boombox. Mum had discovered that there were no groceries in the house even to prepare a light brunch. On Friday, before leaving for work, mum had given Joe a list of things to buy. But as usual he had forgotten all about it. Mum was raging mad that she had no choice but to take us out to lunch.

"Why don't we go to the fancy new Thai restaurant in Mississauga?" said Joe. I couldn't help admiring this guy.

"We're going to the *pho*," mum said, in a chilly no-nonsense voice.

If ever we needed to dine out, mum would always take us to a Vietnamese restaurant on Main Street and order the same dish for each one of us—a noodle soup with meatballs swimming in it. Mum had reckoned that for twenty dollars the three of us could eat our fill and still have some cash leftover for a generous tip.

Hearing about the *pho*, Joe burst out: "I'm sick and tired of eating item no. 18 every time!"

"Really?" mum said.

I recognised that tone. It was only a matter of time before she went all ballistic. The next thing I knew, the two were in the middle of a slanging match. When it was time for Act II, mum threw a punch at Joe. The poor man was taken aback. No woman other than his mum had ever smacked him.

Joe turned and, without a word, crept away went into his basement. He resurfaced twenty minutes later with a suitcase in one hand and a bunch of unwashed clothes in the crook of his other arm. "I'm outta here!" he said and walked out of the house, stopping only to bang the door after him.

The Ford coughed apologetically and refused to start at first. But eventually it did, and emitting a roar, the car sped away. Though I didn't like Joe, I felt kind of sorry for him. Also, a troublesome thought occurred to me—from now I would be mum's main focus. It was something that didn't appeal to me at all. For her part, mum picked up the *Star* and leafed through the entertainment section like it was any other lazy Saturday afternoon.

* * *

And so on my 12th birthday, I saw no signs of any birthday present coming my way. I didn't care either; after all I was in middle school and wasn't a kid anymore. I knew dad would have wanted me to be more responsible, and be protective towards mum. Everyone and their dog knew it was the rest of the humanity that needed shielding from mum.

In the evening we went to the temple in the ancient Chevy Cavalier mum had bought, with expert advice from

Joe, soon after she had learned how to drive. The highway
was buzzing with the summer weekend rush. But I had to
hand it to mum, she drove like a pro. Cohabiting with a
driving instructor seemed to have had its own advantages.

The temple looked the same. But there was a poster on
a wall asking for donations to build a dome.

"It looks like everyone's after my money," mum muttered. "Including God." Then she said something that
alarmed me: "My son comes first; God will have to wait a
little longer." I didn't know what she meant. There was
some talk about braces from my front teeth last year, but it
was costing a packet. I sincerely hoped it wasn't that. What
an idiot I'd look with wires running in my mouth.

On our way back, mum put on the radio. The announcer came on the air, talking about floods in some remote
part of the world. Mum pulled out a small carry bag from
the glove box. Handing me the packet, she said: "Happy
Birthday!"

I was so flabbergasted I forgot to thank her. While she
was listening to the announcer yakking about a mine col-
lapse, I opened the bag and took a peek inside. My eyes
must have surely popped out. An iPod Nano!

Mum shut off the radio, and turned to me. "The things
that happen on your birthday! Floods in Bangladesh, an
accident in a Chinese mine, and a hurricane blowing across
the Caribbean!"

Turning a deaf ear to mum, I opened the package. Sil-
ver-coloured and gleaming, how beautiful the iPod looked!
I was extra careful as I prised out the device. When I held it
in my hands, I was afraid I'd leave indelible fingerprints
behind.

"I think your birthdays are truly jinxed," said mum.

"Me too," I said, absently.

Just for the heck of it, I fished out the earphones and stuffed them into my ears. Though it would be some time before the iPod started pumping music into my ears, I was already beginning to feel happy with my life. I could hardly wait to tell Tony and Mustapha about my birthday present.

"Thank you, mum," I said. "You are the best!"

I wanted to kiss mum on her cheek, but held back because it would have been such an uncool thing to do.

Out of the blue, mum said: "Shall we go out for dinner?"

"Wh-where?" I asked, a vision of meatballs in a foggy soup rising in my mind.

"To the fancy new Thai restaurant in Mississauga," mum said, stepping on the gas.

Ramki and the Christmas Trees

The very first job Ramki got after coming to Canada was to guard a double row of Christmas trees in a city square. In all the livelong years he had spent in India, Ramakrishna, to give Ramki's full name, had seen neither a fir nor a pine, much less a decorated one, complete with ornaments and winking lights.

Ramki and his family had arrived in the spring of that year, and rented a basement apartment in Mississauga. Soon, their dimly-lit and viewless underground home flaunted the smell of curry, like a newly acquired accent. No sooner had they unpacked their enormous suitcases, all six of them, than Ramki started to look for work. He had realised pretty quickly that the money they had brought into the country as "proof of funds" wouldn't last them forever. But however much he tried, he failed to find a job, let alone one in his cherished field of electrical engineering.

"Do you think it will help if I, too, started looking for a job?" his wife asked, despite never having worked in her life.

"I doubt it, Latha. Even if you had a hundred years of experience, it wouldn't matter. They only care for Canadian experience. But what the hell—there's no harm in trying your luck."

Ramki knocked together a one-page resume for Latha on a computer in the local library. Latha went around the nearby malls handing out copies of her resume to the sceptical-looking staff of every shop that had a "Now Hiring" placard stuck on the front window. When she was offered a position as a crew member in a Wendy's outlet, both of them were quite astonished. Latha took the job even though the menu featured beef, an item tabooed by their religion.

But their relief was stillborn.

"Anu's kindergarten class is for half a day only," said Latha. "I can't leave her and go to work."

"I'll look after her when you are away," said Ramki, but his voice belied his optimism.

"No, we must look for a crèche or somebody who can take care of Anu."

"You have a point. I can't stay at home and look for a job at the same time."

When they made enquiries, they found the cost of daycare so astronomical that it made no sense for Latha to surrender almost all of her earnings to a childcare centre. Feeling helpless and frustrated, Ramki decided on an impulse to send Anu back to India to live with her grandparents.

"You don't mean that, do you?" said Latha.

"It will only be a temporary arrangement," Ramki said.

"Even then, living here without Anu is unthinkable for me."

"Life here is not as easy as we had thought, Latha. Neither do we have any relatives here who might give us support."

"We might as well go back to India, if that's the case."

"Latha, I've spent a fortune to immigrate to Canada. We can't return, as if we are failures. Come what may, I'm going to succeed. I'm sure in a couple of years we'll be on our feet again."

The weeks that followed were the most difficult period in Ramki's life. There was an undeclared cold war rife in the house. Latha became moody and taciturn. Often, she seemed to lose herself in a private world which shut Ramki out completely. But Ramki steeled himself; as the head of the family he needed to make difficult choices.

But the most frustrating part was trying to convince Anu.

"In India you can play with all your cousins. You can go to see many films with Grandma. She will cook you all your favourite dishes."

"Will Grandma make me biryani every day?" Anu said.

"Of course!" Ramki said.

"But I don't want to go back to Hyderabad. I want to stay with mummy."

A distant relative living in Winnipeg, who was going with his family on a visit to India, agreed to take Anu along with him.

On the day before Anu's date of departure, when Latha was packing Anu's suitcase, she was overwhelmed with inconsolable grief. Taking her hand, Ramki led Latha away and seated her on the bed. He took over the job of packing, but as he was stuffing Anu's belongings into the bag any which way, he was bitten with a sense of masculine ineptitude— he got the feeling that he was making a hash of the job.

The next day late in the afternoon, they called for a

taxi. They disembarked at Terminal 1, with Ramki dreading the emotional scene he expected to be played out at the security gate. Luckily, his cousin had two girls aged 6 and 8 who kept Anu busy most of the time.

"Be a good girl," said Latha, in a studiedly normal voice for Anu's sake. "Don't trouble Grandma too much, OK?"

The night they returned from the airport, the basement felt like a crypt—cold and deserted.

Lying down by him, Latha was still as a bolster, her heart frozen with misery. Her initial objections had been overcome not by Ramki's reasoning but her own fear of an uncertain future.

"We can bring Anu back, after I find a good job," said Ramki. From the time he decided to send Anu to India, he had been spouting that statement often, like a sporadic geyser.

The still autumnal night, chilly because their landlord was frugal with heating, resonated with Latha's unspoken comment: "As it is, it's so difficult for an immigrant to get a job, how can one ever hope to find a *good* job?"

"I just need an opening, Latha, that's all," said Ramki, as if addressing her thought. "If I work for a couple of years, I can move on to something better, something in my line, hopefully. We must have patience."

* * *

It was seven in the evening when Ramki got into his blue-and-white uniform. Latha had to rush back from Wendy's that afternoon to shorten the legs of the trousers which were designed for Canadian anatomies. Ramki stood at five feet eight, not short by Indian standards. He was thickset, more fat than muscle—but it made him look deceptively strong.

On the evening he was about to leave for work, Latha came to the door and said: "Be careful." She was echoing the disquiet both had felt at the potential dangers of his new job.

Huddling into a heavy coat which had the company's crest emblazoned on the upper arm, Ramki walked down to the bus stop. There were skeins of mist adrift, blurring the street lamps. It had rained wet snow earlier in the day.

When Ramki arrived at the city centre, Murtuza his supervisor was already there, leaning on the door of a patrol car. Murtuza was from Karachi in Pakistan. His grandparents had fled from a town in North India during the Partition.

"Here's the radio," he said, handing Ramki a bulky handset. "You must call the office on the top of every hour. Do you know how to use the radio?"

Without waiting for Ramki to reply, Murtuza pulled out his own radio, and mimicked: "Bravo 12 calling Alpha 2. Ten zero."

The radio bristled in Murtuza's palm, and a response that sounded like someone gargling came through: "Ten two. Ten four."

Murtuza led Ramki to the square in the shadow of the city hall and briefed him about his duties. The place looked gloomier than the rest of the city; the mist having assumed the aspects of a fog, emboldened by the relative openness of the place. It seemed darker too, the only light coming from the Christmas trees, standing at attention like decorated soldiers on either side of a long rectangular pond that was used as an open-air ice rink in winter. A board was put up with the message: "The Rink is Closed." Rain and a sudden spike in temperature had made the rink's top layer soggy.

"Even if the rink opens tomorrow, you don't have to bother yourself with it. Your job is only to guard the Christmas trees."

"Got it," said Ramki. "But what do I guard them from?"

"Some of the trees have been vandalized. All sorts of people visit the square in the night to look at the trees. You should not let them touch the trees or pull out the ornaments."

"Just lookie but no touchie."

"You're right, buddy."

Murtuza left soon afterwards, and Ramki—who had shinnied up trees in the middle of blazing summers to pluck mangoes—began to guard these tall pagoda-like trees which were weighed down not by fruit but a variety of gewgaws.

Ramki plodded up and down the rows as the shimmering trees loomed over him. There were about two dozen conifers, evenly placed at ten-foot intervals. Despite their lights, the trees looked sombre, even secretive. For Ramki, it was a long, lonely vigil, interspersed with bursts of quixotic-sounding broadcasts from his radio. As the hours passed, the trees became more familiar to him, slowly giving up their outlandish quality. He discovered that many of them flaunted ornaments quite unlike the ones on the Christmas trees he had seen in shopping malls. The trees were put up by local organizations, and it gradually dawned on Ramki that they were dressed up to reflect their sponsor's line of business. Along with wisps of traditional ornaments, a music school had hung musical notes cut from golden cardboard; a clothing company, miniature dresses; an auto dealer, model cars; and so on.

The ever-watchful Ramki, radio in hand, patrolled the square with zeal almost religious in its intensity. At around midnight, he saw a dark shape make its way towards the trees. Seized with panic, Ramki radioed his office.

"If he behaves in a dangerous way," said the despatch officer coolly, "*withdraw from the scene.*"

With a palpitating heart, Ramki approached the intruder. The man was a smiling, slightly-drunk patron of a nearby pub who had walked over to see the trees. He gave Ramki a bonhomous wave.

"The trees look neat, eh?"

"Yes," said Ramki, alert to any exhibition of dangerous behaviour.

The man went around showing his admiration by spitting expletives like 'Holy shit!' and 'Aw shucks' before disappearing into the night, without either ravaging the decorations or shooting Ramki point-blank. Ramki sighed with relief. Every day on TV he heard of people getting shot or knifed.

At around half past one, a young man turned up and sat down on a bench out in the open. When Ramki walked past him, the young man started a conversation. He was a short-order cook who worked in a steakhouse down the road, and was on his way home.

"Man, I've never seen the likes of them before," said the young man, pointing at the trees. "Is this the first time they're doing this?"

"I don't know," Ramki said, wishing he knew how to be friendly to a perfect stranger in the dead of the night. The man left after lounging in the cold for about half an hour. Ramki couldn't help wondering what made a young man hang around in a cold, empty city square rather than go home to a warm bed. Didn't he have anyone waiting for him? He thought of his own home, of Latha, and then when his thoughts turned to Anu, he felt a twinge of longing.

The night passed without any mishaps, and all the Christmas trees remained inviolate. At five in the morning, Ramki sighed with relief—a relief tinged with a feeling of triumph. Ramki, whose working life had been dedicated to motors, carbon brushes and armatures, had successfully coped with the strangest assignment he had ever been offered. He called the office on the radio and booked off.

As he walked to the bus stop at a corner of the square, a small wind started to blow and it got noticeably colder. Trembling in the glass-walled bus shelter, which hosted an ad for cruises to the Caribbean, he waited for what seemed like ages for the first bus of the day. When he reached home, a sleepy Latha asked him if he'd like to have a cup of coffee. Ramki preferred to go to bed straightaway. He wanted to catch enough sleep so that he could face another workday night. Living life one night at a time, he told himself. This was a temporary job which would end the moment they took down the trees. But Ramki wanted to make a good impression; Murtuza had hinted that if he did his job well there was a chance of something more permanent.

He woke up around noon to a throbbing head. He swallowed two Tylenols, hoping the headache would subside before he left for work. Latha was at home and he could smell the chicken curry she was making for him.

When he finished his lunch, a kind of lethargy stole over him. He was lolling on the bed when Latha came over and lay down beside him. She was in her late twenties, light-skinned, and pretty with finely-chiselled features. But worry and overwork were taking their toll: the sharp outlines of her face were starting to blur. Her complexion looked sallow, Ramki had noticed, without *kohl* around her eyes and *tikka* on her forehead. Latha had stopped using traditional make-up after coming to Canada. Ramki turned on his side and put his arm round her.

"How's your headache?" Latha said.

Picking up a small vial of Amrutanjan from the bedside table, she applied a pinch of the sickly-yellow pain balm on his forehead. Both Ramki and Latha had been amazed to learn that familiar Indian products like Bru coffee, Pond's talcum powder, and Brahmi hair oil, to say nothing of Amrutanjan, were available in Toronto, even if only at Indian grocery shops. As Latha rubbed his temple, she said: "Can I ask you something?"

"What is it?"

"Now that you've got a job, can we bring Anu back?"

"Latha, yesterday was the first day at my new job! I don't even know if I'll last out all the 20 days they promised me. Working in the night during winters is no joke."

"I know. But we were in too much of a hurry to send Anu back. There are so many immigrant families living here, and not all of them have good jobs. Somehow, they manage to stay together. Maybe with the help of the government child support, we too can do it."

"Child support! Are we beggars? Anyway, it's such a measly sum. Now that I've got this job, it would reduce even further, I'm sure."

"I heard there are private Indian babysitters. And their rates are very reasonable—they charge only a couple of dollars an hour. If we look around we'll be able to find one."

"Latha, the job I have is a temporary one," Ramki said. "Once the Christmas holidays are over I might not have it."

"You don't seem to understand—"

"I do. I left a good job and came over here. I'll do anything, anything, to make a success of it."

"But it's not a good thing for our child to grow up so far away from us."

"Anu's staying with my parents, not with some Indian babysitters! We'll discuss about Anu, only after I get a permanent job, all right? I want to take some rest now." And he turned his back on her.

He heard the swish of Latha's nightgown, as she got up and walked away. The headache tightened like a steel belt around his skull. He wondered angrily whether he would get any sleep at all. He need not have feared—without his knowing, he fell asleep.

Later in the evening, when he left for work, Latha came to the front door. He bent down to kiss her but she averted her face.

* * *

When Ramki arrived at the city square, the place looked as if it had been subjected to an extreme make-over. He couldn't believe his eyes: streamers of coloured lights were suspended over the reopened rink, and catchy dance music was being played loudly. The atmosphere was festive, and the scene glowed with the brilliant purity of a water-colour.

A Zamboni prowled on the ice, leaving behind a trail of glaze. There were dozens of people, many of them wearing skates, sitting on benches or standing about, waiting for the Zamboni to finish its job. The Christmas trees on either side of the rink shone with a soft friendly glow, and looked convivial as though enjoying the company of the young, lively throng. When the Zamboni heaved itself out, the skaters returned to the rink *en masse*, and egged on by the music from the loudspeakers, began to circumambulate the frozen pond with a single-minded devotion.

Ramki called his office to book on and began his patrol. He found a few ornaments lying on the ground, which had been apparently torn off the trees. He tied them back on to their respective trees. One of the ornaments he restored was a small plastic frame containing a picture of a smiling boy with a missing front tooth. The picture reminded Ramki of Anu; he wondered whether she had lost her first tooth by now. He had no idea at what age children lost their milk teeth. Latha would know. He must remember to ask her.

It was almost eleven when the last of the skaters left. Once the rink was empty, the lights and music were shut off. The temperature seemed to drop a couple of degrees in the silent darkness. The trees reacquired their secretive look, and whispered conspiratorially to one another whenever the wind hurried through them.

All through the freezing night, the trees—shining like beacons—attracted visitors, mostly stragglers from the Irish pub. A majority of them would just wander about—like tourists who are not particularly passionate about paintings in an art gallery—before the cold made them leave the place.

It was one thirty in the night when a triad of young men appeared in the square. Pleasantly drunk, they joked among themselves, as they took a tour of the caparisoned trees. They lingered at the tree that boasted model cars, fingering the decorations.

Ramki walked up to them and said: "Gentlemen, no touching." For some reason, they looked at each other and laughed uproariously.

"Sorry, bro," said one of them, and the trio left soon afterwards "As their bantering faded into the night, Ramki smiled ruefully. How long it had been since he had partied with such abandon? Nowadays, Latha was never in a mood to socialize with the few friends they had made after coming over.

After two o'clock there were few visitors, and a pall of quietness settled over the square. As Ramki made his rounds, clutching the radio in his hand, his mind went back to the tiff he had had with Latha that afternoon. He felt his annoyance returning. Did she really think that he did not love Anu? How could he explain to her that, if he did not get a well-paying job, they too would have to go back to India? Was it possible to work all your life in a warehouse or a takeaway—those were the places where most of the openings were—and hope to make it big? Sometimes he could not understand Latha at all.

He remembered the times when he had cradled Anu —smelling of mother's milk and Johnson's Baby Powder —gingerly in his hands, careful to provide support to her tender neck. Every time he carried her in his arms, he had felt his heart bloom like a flower with love. But he had grown up believing that a man's primary duty was to safe-guard and provide for his family. Didn't his concern for their financial security qualify as love?

Often he had been short with Latha, not meaning to be rude. He must have come off as being unkind, even un-caring. How ironic—when the future of his family was all he had in his mind. Sending Anu away was a purely tempor-ary measure—a way of buying time to put their finances on a sounder footing. Why couldn't Latha see that?

Immigration was serious business, he had learned. It was not a ticket to success; it demanded hardship and sac-rifice. He was prepared to face the challenges. The only other alternative—he wouldn't even consider it for a mo-ment!—was for all of them to return to India, like losers.

As he paced up and down the rows, thinking things out, he had to acknowledge that Latha, as a mother, might have her own point of view. Perhaps he had been unfair to her. Could he make amends by showing her more sympa-thy? How could he defuse the situation? The domestic dis-harmony was getting on his nerves, and it would surely get in the way of his dream to succeed in Canada.

It was three in the morning. Diligently, he radioed his office to make his customary report.

Without Anu even his home seemed dull and lifeless, and this had nothing to do with Latha's periodic bouts of silence. When he made the harsh and unpopular decision, he had never suspected that he would miss Anu so much.

As Ramki loitered in the lonely square, strongly vivid images of his daughter came to his mind: her laughter at nothing in particular, sounding like small, joyous bells; her

frequent but short-lived wailing to have her way; her running up to him, her arms raised to signal she wished to be
carried.

A handsome couple walked into the square, shaking
Ramki out of his reverie. It was half past three. It struck
even Ramki, untrained as he was in the subject of fashion,
that the woman was smartly turned out—dressed in a natty
dark-coloured coat and boots to match. A wealth of golden
tresses gushed down to her shoulders from under her beret-
like cap. Wearing only a short skirt and stockings, she was
unmindful of the cold. Her companion was handsome in
a craggy way, like men in ads for aftershaves. The woman
smiled and the man nodded as they passed him. The
woman stopped by every tree, and looked at the ornaments
as though she were studying them. She read every placard
tacked on to the trees while the man beside her looked
on, bored.

Ramki shadowed them, radio in hand—just in case.

"What a remarkable tree!" the woman exclaimed. When
she saw Ramki bearing down upon them, she said: "You'd
have already seen it."

"Seen what?" Ramki said.

The tree was the last one in its row. He had not observed it closely because he would always turn around before he came abreast with it. But he remembered that last
night he put back an ornament that had fallen off from it.
This time round, he examined the tree more closely. There
were ornaments of all sorts, and nestling among them were
framed photographs of children—scores of them. Some
smiling, some bashful, all of them so sweet, all of them so

angelic. How proud their parents must be of them, thought Ramki. He was reminded of Anu once again.

He looked at the placard—the tree was put up by an organisation that provided child services. Even as he was reading about the theme, he heard the woman gasp: "These are photographs of children who have gone missing! How shocking! The poor mothers!"

She turned to look at her beau and Ramki, and added: "How terrible it must be to have your child snatched from you."

In the light from the Christmas trees, Ramki saw her eyes glint with tears. Did she herself lose a child? Or was it just empathy for the unfortunate parents? A gust of wind blew, and the doleful tree, crowded with pictures of luckless little children, trembled.

Ramki too was overwhelmed with a sense of loss. He thought of Anu and Latha—and he had so wilfully separated them. In the cold dark night, as he stood by the tree, in his heart he understood his wife.

Demon Glass

The one open eye, looking so much larger than its fellow, followed Lalita as she walked across the living room carrying the letters she had plucked out of her shared mailbox. Lalita was in her late thirties and, without any conscious effort on her part, she'd retained her natural good looks—her full figure, raven-black hair and those dreamy almond-shaped eyes.

Lalita threw the bills and flyers on to the study table that stood in for a dining table at meal times. Sinking into a couch that had lost its shape and colour even before it had turned up at a garage sale, Lalita began to tear open the only letter—an actual handwritten one—that had come that day.

Neela, her 11-year-old daughter, put down the magnifying glass to see all the more clearly. She asked: "Who is it from, mother?"

"Pari-aunty," Lalita said. "Do you remember her?"

"Y-yes," Neela said.

Lalita began to read the letter, squinting in the dim light of her basement apartment. Parijatam's shaky, old-fashioned hand did not make the task any lighter. Parijatam and Lalita had worked together as teachers at a secondary school in India.

The letter was a mixture of sympathy for Lalita (for being so far away from her friends and relatives) and self-pity for Parijatam herself (for being only too close to *her* friends and relatives). An enigmatic smile appeared on Lalita's lips when she read the sentence: "Life must be so lonely for you in Canada."

After she finished reading the letter, Lalita asked her daughter: "What will you have for dinner?"

Neela was crawling on the floor peering at various objects in a Sherlockian manner. She was a lanky child who looked like a scaled down model of her mother. She said: "Dosas."

"You had them only the other day."

"Daddy used to have dosas everyday."

"Nonsense," Lalita said. "What do you remember of him?" Or I, for that matter, Lalita said to herself. Neela had been only four when Prasad and she separated.

No matter what Neela said she'd have for dinner, Lalita invariably pulled out small boxes of leftovers from the fridge, and re-heated them.

When the microwave stopped beeping, Lalita removed the punished-looking Rubbermaid dishes and set them on the table. "Dinner's ready," she announced, like a hostess in a TV show.

Neela whipped out her magnifying glass and inspected the fare.

"I'm not hungry," she said.

"Stop making a fuss," Lalita said, "and eat your dinner!"

"I said I'm not hungry, OK?"

"It's not OK! You'll have to eat something. Everyone says you're so skinny."

"Who says so?"

"Prem-Uncle, for one."

"I don't like Prem-Uncle."

"Eat," said Lalita said "And not another word."

* * *

The following afternoon, Lalita stood in the shade of the gigantic 'M', outside the McDonalds in Malton. She was now reconciled to working in a fast food restaurant; she had found the lengthy process of first getting her credentials verified and then working indefinitely as a supply teacher too daunting.

An endless procession of cars scurried past while her restless eyes scanned the road for Prem's burgundy-coloured Nissan. Lalita looked at her watch. It was past four and Neela would be home by now. Fortunately for Lalita, Mrs. Rao, her landlady, hailed from the same part of India and spoke the same language. The good woman did not mind taking in Neela for a couple of hours, if Lalita was delayed on account of overtime or otherwise. (Otherwise being a euphemism for Prem-Uncle.)

Prem's car rounded the corner and approached her, winking blearily. It halted in front of her, and Prem leaned across the passenger seat to open the door for her. "Jump in. Quick!" he said. He was in his mid-thirties and attractive, even though there was a residue of teenage acne on his face, and his muscles of late were turning into flab.

Lalita scrambled into the car, smuggling in an unmistakable aroma of Big Mac with her. Even as she was trying to strap the seat belt on, Prem pulled her towards him and tried to kiss her.

"Stop!" Lalita said, searching for the buckle of the seatbelt.

"I missed you so much, darling!" Prem said, attempting to nuzzle her.

"Stop it, I said. Not here!"

"How like a schoolmarm you sound."

They were on their way to Prem's house in Brampton. His wife Vanaja worked at a lawyer's office in downtown Toronto. She commuted by Go Train and came home late in the evening. Prem claimed that he worked as a "job-developer". Lalita never understood what Prem did for a living, but she couldn't help admiring his resourcefulness at finding a job which seemingly had no fixed hours of work.

Prem and Vanaja were the only people Lalita had known in Canada when she arrived as an immigrant, a single mother with a nine-year-old daughter in tow. Vanaja had been a college classmate of Lalita's younger sister in Bangalore. When Lalita called Vanaja from a payphone, the latter's response was both enthusiastic and welcoming. Vanaja helped Lalita in every way to settle down in an alien land. And Prem, not be outdone, began to help Lalita—in ways his wife wouldn't have approved.

"We're moving," said Prem, interrupting Lalita's thoughts. She looked out of the window in confusion.

"I'd think so!" she said.

"I mean, Van and I are moving to another house."

"Not again!"

"The place is close to where Van works."

"So soon? You didn't tell me that you were planning to move." It seemed like it was only the other day that Prem and Vanaja had bought their town house and moved out of a basement apartment very similar to the one she was living in: sans sunlight, sans fresh air, but with an overabundance of vermin.

"It all happened in a rush," he said. "It was too good a deal for me to give up. Van says it comes from being a Scorpio."

"What does?" Lalita asked.

"Having an eye for a good bargain."

"I'll second that," Lalita said.

"What's your sign, by the way?"

"Virgo," she said, primly.

"You?" Prem said with a chuckle. "Don't tell me!"

They drove in silence for some time. Lalita was seized with a feeling of desolation. People she knew were always moving up or moving away, but she would remain stuck forever in her basement.

"You're moving on purpose," Lalita spat out all of a sudden. "I know you're tired of me."

"What are you saying?" Prem said.

"You're trying to shake me off ..."

"Why do you say that? If my house is too far away, we can always meet at your place."

"That's impossible."

"Well ..." Prem started to say. Lalita could almost hear him say, beggars can't be choosers. Changing his tone, Prem said: "Cheer up. It won't be all that bad."

He switched on the stereo. The car was at once filled

with heavy bass notes. Prem liked his music real loud, especially while making love. He patted Lalita's knee, and then his dark hand, looking so much like a cobra, began to crawl up her thigh.

* * *

When Lalita did not hear from Prem for a whole month, she began to feel uneasy—even though she knew that moving was no mean task. When she did receive a phone call, it was from Vanaja, inviting her to the housewarming party. But Lalita found the prospect of seeing Vanaja in person uncomfortable.

"Sorry, Vanaja," Lalita said. "You'll have to excuse me. Apart from the distance, I have to go to work in the evening on that day."

Lalita had almost given up Prem for lost when one day —after what seemed like years—she received a call from him.

"Did you miss me?" Prem said.

"Trust me, I managed quite well without you."

"I'll pick you up in the evening today," he said. "We'll go to your place."

"OK," said Lalita so readily that she herself was surprised.

In the evening, as they drove to her house, Lalita said: "Neela's birthday is coming up soon."

"Great," said Prem. "How old will she be?"

"Twelve."

"Soon she'll be a young woman, eh?" said Prem. "And a beauty like her mother, I guess."

"Stop it."

"What would she like to have for her birthday?"

Last year, Prem had given Neela a stamp collector's kit. Ignoring the assortment of stamps altogether, Neela had taken an instant fancy to the magnifying glass that came with the set.

When Lalita referred to it using an Indian word, Neela had said: "What's that, Mother?"

"*Boothaddam*," Lalita had repeated. "It means demon glass."

"Demon glass ..." Neela enunciated dreamily, as if enchanted by the sound of the words.

"This year," Lalita said to Prem, "she wants a microscope."

Prem couldn't stop himself from laughing, "What a peculiar wish! I'd think she'd badger you for a cell phone or make-up kit or something like that."

When they reached Lalita's house, they found Neela playing by herself: she was examining a creepy-crawly with her magnifying glass.

The connecting door between the basement and the owner's portion was open. Lalita said loudly and with elaborate formality: "Thank you for the ride. Can I make you a cup of tea?"

Prem gave her a look of surprise, but said gamely: "Sounds like a good idea."

Lalita went up to the door and shut it.

"Look who has come!" Lalita said to her daughter.

Neela was silent.

"Prem-Uncle!" Lalita gushed, as if wanting to stir up some excitement. "Say hello to uncle."

"Hello" said Neela aid.

"Hi, kiddo," Prem said. "So you want to become a detective, eh?"

"No," Neela said. "An entomologist."

"A doctor! Wow!"

"I'll make some tea," Lalita said, hurriedly.

"Can I have a look too?" said Prem said to Neela. He took the magnifying glass proffered by Neela, and went down on his knees to examine the bug. "Looks quite scary close up," he said. He returned the lens, and mussed Neela's hair.

"Neela, why don't you go outside and play? I'll call you when the tiffin is ready."

Neela picked up her magnifying glass, and walked out of the basement. Prem went up to the stereo system and played a tape of Hindi film songs, and turned up the volume. Lalita switched off the light, and before anyone could say 'Prem-Uncle', they were rolling on the couch in the surreal darkness of her basement, forgetting all about tea and tiffin. When they finished their business, Lalita rolled out of the couch and got up. As she was putting on her clothes, she let out a gasp.

"What's the matter?" Prem asked.

She was staring at the small window high up in the wall. She said: "I saw somebody looking in."

"You're imagining things."

"No. It must have been Neela!"

"Don't get excited unnecessarily. What could she have seen in this darkness? Even if she did, it's time she learnt the facts of life."

"Don't talk about Neela in that tone. She's still a child."

"That's what you think. Girls in Canada grow up fast."

Lalita was silent for some time. Then she said: "I don't think it's a good idea to meet here."

Getting into his trousers, Prem said: "It's up to you."

* * *

It's spring, and the last of the snow has melted away. There are bird calls all around and the trees are in bud. Lalita too has turned over a new leaf. She has put her affair with Prem behind her, wishing to move on with her life. She's had enough of men's caprices—they want all the fun without the responsibility. It's time she began to think of Neela's future.

On a couple of occasions in the past, Neela told her that Prem-Uncle had phoned. But Lalita had refused to call back. Yet, one evening while walking up from the bus stop, she had seen what looked like Prem's reddish-brown car whiz past her on the street where she lives. She had rushed to the house, as fast as her legs could carry her and demanded, breathlessly, of Neela: "Was Prem-Uncle here?"

Neela looking up from her homework had said, with unwarranted sharpness: "No! But why are you asking?"

"It's nothing," she had said weakly, engulfed with disappointment.

Now that Neela is 12 and can be left alone in the house, Lalita has begun to work longer hours. She has also started attending night classes, hoping to land an office job. As to that incident where she saw someone looking in through the window, Lalita has simply shut it out of her mind, like it never happened.

Nowadays, her apartment has begun to look cleaner and somehow brighter. You can always find Downy-fresh clothes in the chest of drawers. The fridge holds fruits and vegetables besides leftovers.

"Yet," Lalita tells herself, as she vacuums the bedroom floor, "Everyone seems to have turned against me, now."

That's true. Neela has grown a little stubborn of late, and is doing poorly at school. Even more puzzling is Mrs. Rao's behaviour. To all of Lalita's polite enquiries, she responds with a sullen "hmpf". Surely it cannot be because Neela has begun to shut the connecting door between their basement and the landlady's portion of the house?

The hoover begins to splutter, as if something is stuck in its throat. Lalita bends down and prises out a metallic object from the machine. It is a silver bracelet bearing an engraving: *From Van with Love, 11-04-2007.*

"Eleventh of April. Must be Prem's birthday."

Though she has never seen the ornament before, it triggers an upsurge of passion within her. She can almost feel Prem's presence—sweaty and smelling of Old Spice—in the room. She shakes herself free from the clutches of her emotions, marches determinedly to the kitchen and throws the bracelet in the garbage.

Humming a tune to herself rather loudly, as if to show her nonchalance, Lalita resumes her vacuuming. She spots a millipede crawling on the carpet, but the hoover gobbles it up without a hiccup.

"At least these bugs are not as bad as the scorpions back home …"

Lalita freezes, the song dies on her lips and the vacuum cleaner begins to protest loudly.

"Prem is a Scorpio. I remember his saying so. So the date on the bracelet must be fourth of November. We broke up in September. How could the bracelet have gotten under the bed?"

The doorbell rings insistently, interrupting Lalita's train of thoughts. She shuts off the vacuum cleaner and goes to the front door. Mrs. Rao is on the doorstep looking more sullen than usual.

"H-hi," Lalita says, unsure of what to expect.

"Hmpf. I've been meaning to tell you something."

"Please go ahead."

"Nowadays, Neela plays the stereo very loudly, and it disturbs Mr. Rao's afternoon nap."

"Neela isn't like that," Lalita says. "Besides, she's not fond of music."

"Then it must be the baby-sitter."

"What baby-sitter? What are you talking about?"

"Your friend. The guy who comes in a maroon car."

"Burgundy, actually," Lalita hears herself say, her mind busy piecing together the mental jigsaw.

"Maybe, but he's here very often," her landlady says.

"Oh, my God!" Lalita's legs seem to give way and she has to lean back against the wall.

"Are you all right?" When Lalita does not reply, she adds: "You don't look good. Would you like to come in for a cup of tea?"

"No, no. I'm OK," Lalita says, turning to leave.

"Take care of yourself, dear," Mrs. Rao says, withdrawing into her house.

Covering her face with her palms, Lalita sobs. Alone in her grief.

Going West

When the airplane banked, Toronto's sprawl swung into view and I had my first glimpse of the CN Tower, rising like an upended middle-finger. The huge butterflies in my stomach were only growing bigger.

The aircraft swooped down and, landing with a thud, raced down the runway hell bent for leather. But as if having thought better of it, the plane slowed down and eventually came to a stop. Soon afterwards some of the passengers shot up like jack-rabbits and dashed to the exit, clogging the aisles. I waited for the line up to subside before I got up from my seat and pulled out my hand luggage from the overhead rack. Dragging the bag after me, and balancing a rather capacious coat on my arm, I sidled out of the plane. I clutched the coat—the thickest I could buy in India—as if it were some sort of talisman that would protect me from Canada's notorious cold.

After a long trek though a seemingly endless corridor, I waited in a cavernous hall with a planeload of landed immigrants—men, women and their cranky children. When my number was called I entered a small cell. The border official took my Indian passport and the snot-green landing paper, and checked every line in them, periodically looking up to examine my face so intently that I half-expected him to whip out a pair of handcuffs and slap them onto my wrists. But he was more interested in the "proof of funds" I had brought with me. Satisfied with the loot, he said: "Welcome to Canada!"

I collected my oversized bags, and stood in the lobby of Pearson International Airport, sweeping my searching gaze in a semicircle over the multicultural collection of faces of people waiting for their near and dear to emerge. Some in the crowd had surgical masks tied to their faces—I remembered reading in the papers about flu outbreaks in Toronto. Praful Patel, the owner of the guesthouse I'd be staying at, had promised to receive me—for a fee, of course. There was a fair sprinkling of south Asians, but I managed to lock on his unsure, half-smiling face. He looked older than in the JPEG image he'd emailed me.

A few days before leaving for Canada, I had surfed the Internet looking for some sort of accommodation that wouldn't be too expensive. Checking into a hotel was out of the question. As to friends and relatives in Canada, I had none. On the web I found a not so flattering review of the Patel guesthouse. It was a pension-like set up where immigrants could avail themselves of its frugal hospitality without getting gouged. I'm not the type to give much credence to all the reviews one encounters on the net, so I booked myself a spot—I was thankful to have an inexpensive place to go to, straight from the airport.

Praful extended his hand and said: "Welcome to Canada. Did you have a pleasant journey?"

Taking his hand, I nodded—though I wouldn't call travelling 20,000 miles in 24 hours with two extended lay-overs and not much sleep, *pleasant*.

Praful took control of the trolley and we walked to the parking lot. The spring evening was bright but it still had a nip to it. I hugged my overcoat a little tighter. Praful, who was dressed in a golf shirt and shorts, seemed impervious to the weather. Once the suitcases were stowed in the trunk, I went around and stood on what I thought was the passenger side. Praful too materialized on the same side.

"Sorry! I forgot you drive on the wrong side in this country!" I said.

"No problem. There are many things in this country which are the exact opposite of what you find in India. You'll get used to them."

During the 20-minute drive to his semi-detached house in Mississauga, Praful played Bollywood songs for my benefit. The Patels ran their guesthouse out of this property.

"Every Sunday they show a Hindi movie on TV," he said. "But if you have a satellite dish, there's no limit to how many Indian movies you can see! Do you like Hindi movies?"

"No," I said. I didn't mean to offend him. In India I had watched Hollywood films in regular theatres, and enjoyed old French cinema shown at special screenings even more.

"Oh!" Praful said. "Should I switch off the music?"

"No, don't!" I said. "I like Hindi film music."

The houses on the street he lived had a uniform appearance with chocolate brown façades and lawns the size of living room carpets. Praful taxied the car close to the front door. Between the two of us, we managed to move the oversized suitcases into the lobby. When I pushed open the front door, I was at once assailed by the stale aroma of Indian cooking. I had not experienced such a powerful bouquet even in India where a billion mouths fed on Indian cuisine every day.

A plump middle-aged woman, with close-cropped hair and dressed in shirt and pants, came forward and said: "I'm Mrs. Patel. Welcome to Canada."

All the Mrs. Patels I had met hitherto had worn saris, even if wrong way round in Gujju style. Mrs. Patel unwittingly delivered the first jolt of culture shock to an immigrant from India. Maybe, reading the astonishment on my face, and perhaps wanting to calm me, she added hurriedly: "I'll make some chai for you. Sit down and relax."

No sooner had she gone into the kitchen than a man came down the large wooden staircase that seemed to dominate the living room area. He was of medium height and light-skinned. Though he had a pleasant face, a faint grimace hovered over his lips. His gaze was piercing and his eyes restlessly moved around noting everything in the vicinity.

Praful introduced us: "Kumar meet our new guest. He's from Hyderabad."

"Welcome to Canada," Kumar said without enthusiasm, and added: "I want to speak to Falguni."

The man went into the kitchen and at once started remonstrating with Mrs. Patel. I could hear the argument over the timpani of the kitchen utensils.

"Falguni, why should I pay for the lock?"

"Because you've lost the key!"

"I only lost the key, not the lock!"

"Kumar, you are not exactly a newcomer to Canada, you should know how things are done here."

"Of course I do, only too well, but I don't like the idea of coughing up hundred and fifty dollars to replace a door-lock."

I was bit stunned myself. I instantly converted the amount to Indian rupees, and it came to nearly ten thousand rupees, a big sum back home. I was quite aware before I left India that going West was no passport to prosperity. Even then.

Praful got up and said to me: "Come on, I'll take you to your room."

As we climbed the stairs, lugging my suitcases, Praful cautioned me, using only gestures, to tread quietly. I noticed then that, unlike back home, staircases and floors in Canadian homes were constructed of wood which made a noise unless you trod gingerly.

The room upstairs was little more than a box, and had two cots set at right angles. I could make out the spoor of the other occupant: a shirt hanging on the back of a chair, a used coffee mug on a table, the odour of unwashed socks.

It was getting dark, so I reached out my hand and tried to switch on the light. I found the toggle switch already at "on" position.

"Aren't the lights working?" I asked.

Switching on the light, Praful said: "You must push it up to put on the light."

In India the electrical switches operated in the opposite way. It was at this moment, standing awash in the yellow light of low wattage, that it dawned on me that I had left my own country for good and immigrated to a land about which I knew so very little.

"Dinner will be served until 9 o'clock," Praful said, as he handed me a stapled sheaf of paper—an exhaustive list of do's and don'ts for guests.

After a quick bath, I lay down on the cot with the virgin bedcover and began to read the house rules—it was a kind of community manifesto authored by Praful himself.

It included such helpful hints as "Do not pass urine in standing position," a practice I decided to embrace the next time I went to the loo. As I was wending though the list item by item (there was one prohibiting the guests from throwing used toilet paper in the bathroom trash can), I fell asleep, overcome by jetlag.

* * *

The Patels, who occupied the master bedroom, were sixtyish and their two married daughters lived in the USA. My roomie Naveen, in his mid-20's like me, was another new immigrant. An engineer and an expert in ball bearings, he was indefatigably seeking a job appropriate to his education and work experience, like a knight searching for the Holy Grail (and with as little success). The third bedroom was occupied by Kumar who appeared to do nothing other than wallow in idleness. Naveen called him "The Prince," not so much because his first name was Yuvraj, but more for his lordly ways and an unconcern with the fears that usually beset a new immigrant.

The next morning, I lounged in the solarium reading the *Mississauga News* after a breakfast of cold toast with No

Name margarine and jam. I would soon discover that the breakfast was the same every day, only the flavour of the jam changing. If it's Tuesday, it must be strawberry, if it's Wednesday it must be raspberry …

The Prince was in the solarium too, enthroned on a chair, twiddling his thumbs.

"Kumar," said Falguni, bustling into the room. "Let's go."

Only moments ago, while slapping a swathe of jam (blueberry as it was a Saturday) on to his toast, the Prince had volunteered to accompany her to buy the weekly groceries.

"I'm not coming," he said. "I've to call a hiring agency."

"Fine," Falguni said, obviously accustomed to his habit of flip-flopping. "Just so you know, the hiring agency will be closed today." Without waiting to hear the convoluted explanation he offered, she left.

Naveen entered the room, wiping the crumbs of toast from his mouth. The Prince said with a touch of sarcasm: "Found a suitable job, Naveen?"

"No."

"I know of many engineers," The Prince said, "who have years of experience working for multinationals, but haven't been able to get a decent job in Canada. They're working as labourers, poor fellers."

Naveen's face darkened. I could sense the chill that entered his heart as palpably as the cold you feel when you open a freezer door. He had forsaken a secure, well-paid job to immigrate to Canada.

"Get yourself a Canadian degree," The Prince said. "Then you'll find something in your line."

"Isn't university education expensive?"

"Not very," The Prince said with his typical nonchalance.

"It's only a matter of twenty thousand dollars a year or so."

"Twenty K!" Naveen exclaimed. "How can I raise such a sum?"

"What about OSAP?" I suggested, having done my homework before leaving India.

"OSAP!" The Prince said, looking outraged. "You can apply for the student loan *only* after you have spent a year in Ontario."

The Prince turned on me, having seen me comb through the "situation vacant" column.

"Don't waste your time on newspaper ads," he said. "Nobody's going to call you for an interview. The employers want Canadian experience."

"A dynamo in India is no different from a dynamo in Canada," Naveen said. "I don't understand the importance given to Canadian experience."

"Nobody does," The Prince said. "You should approach an employment agency. They pay about 12 dollars an hour for factory jobs."

Did he think I came halfway across the globe to work as general labour? The Prince was aware that I had held a middle level position in HR in India. Granted finding a similar job in Canada was next to impossible (thanks to different labour laws and employment standards) but surely there were other white-collared openings available? Talking to the Prince was so dispiriting, especially if you were a newcomer to the country. He was not the best buddy to have in a cold, lonely land. The Prince could have unravelled even Penelope's fabled resolve in a blink.

The Prince pressed on: "All the new jobs are in Alberta. They have a severe shortage of labour, and the salaries there are astronomical. Counter help at Tim Hortons gets 18 dollars an hour. You should think of moving to Calgary or Edmonton."

I got up to leave the room—I had had enough of Kumar's crash course on survival in Canada for the day.

"Where are you going?" The Prince asked.

"I have a call to make."

I didn't tell him it was nature's call.

* * *

It's my belief that, if a sculptor were commissioned to create the image of an immigrant, he'd be better advised to avoid the carpet-bagger kind of figure, and fashion something like Rodin's *Thinker* but with the classified section of a newspaper open on his lap. Not finding employment is the immigrant's greatest worry.

Ignoring The Prince's suggestion, I sprayed and prayed—in the job-hunter's lingo it meant, you scattered your resumes indiscriminately and waited for the Almighty to do his bit. Though not the best thing to do, in my case it worked. I snagged a job in a telemarketing firm which required me to call unsuspecting customers in the USA, and sell them an overpriced, out-of-date business directory.

It was time now for me to leave the guesthouse, which was just a watering place where immigrants made their first landfall. Though the place had so many shortcomings when compared to a hotel, it had a charming familial atmosphere. While it was true that Praful and Falguni ran the place in a casual manner, they more than made up by helping the newcomers, in their avuncular fashion, to navigate

the unknown terrain of immigration. Many a new immigrant carried fond memories of how readily the Patels gave
their advice on how to apply for a health card, or open a
bank account, or look for employment. When The Prince
came to know of my intention, he said: "A basement apartment can be dicey. I read in the papers that a family living
in a basement died of carbon monoxide poisoning."

"How horrible," I said. "But what makes you think I'll
be renting a basement apartment?"

"Come to think of it, you should go in for a house.
Mortgage rates are at a historical low."

"Really? I didn't know that."

"Even if you buy a semi you can sublet the basement to
pay off the mortgage."

"I'll keep that in mind, Kumar, when I plan to buy a
piece of real estate for myself. Right now I'd like to concen-
trate on my new job."

* * *

In the same week, Naveen too found work—a job worthy of
an engineer, even if the salary wasn't. It was contract work
at an auto-ancillary factory in Oshawa. Naveen was offered
$15 an hour, a figure any newcomer to Canada would barter
his soul for. Naveen was most deserving of the break; he
was sincere and persevering, and maintained a network of
friends and contacts, and had used them to good account.

"The first thing to do is to get yourself a car," The
Prince told Naveen, buttonholing him one afternoon. "Even
a pre-owned would do."

"I've never heard of that make," Naveen said.

"It's not a make," I said. "He means a second-hand car."

"Oh. It sounds like a German name. I don't even have a licence. Why should I bother myself now about what kind of car I should buy?"

"Did you drive a car in India?" the Prince said, refusing to be deflected. "If not, you'll have to wait for a year after you pass the written test."

"No, I had a motorcycle," Naveen said. "But my licence was for both, motorcycle and car."

"Then there's nothing to worry. I advise you to take the road test in Burlington or St Catherine's—you can get licences faster there."

"What about Brampton?" I said.

"If I were you, I'd avoid it like plague," he said, and then suddenly glanced at his watch.

The word plague must have reminded him of his need to hit the road. His fear of new strains of viruses being reported in the press made him reluctant to use public transit. If he was ever required to take a bus he put on a nose mask, which he kept in readiness in his back pocket, like some people keep condoms.

"Hell! I have an appointment at 3 o'clock," The Prince said. He added in a voice tinged with relief: "I doubt if I'll be able to make it."

"You'll surely make it," Falguni said, having just entered the room. "Even if you are going to be late, you'd better go. You can think up of some excuse. They see dozens of applicants for labour jobs, they'll not mind if you are late by a few minutes."

"What makes you think it's a labour job?" The Prince asked. "It's in the quality control department at Maple Plastics."

"Don't try to fool me. I know Maple Plastics. Quite a few of our guests have found work in that factory. You can call it Quality Control if you like, but your work will be to weed out misshaped plastic items from a conveyor belt."

"Anyway, it's not like lifting hundreds of pounds in a warehouse all day," The Prince said, standing up and pulling out a mask from his back pocket, like an outlaw in a Western drawing out his derringer.

"Funny guy," Naveen said, after The Prince had left. "I'm puzzled why he hasn't been able to find a job."

"He finds jobs," Falguni said. "His problem is he doesn't stick to them."

"He is such a fund of information, though," Naveen said.

"What has he been telling you?"

"He gave us some advice about how to get a driver's license."

"It's surprising that he should be talking about licences. He has never applied for one, though Praful and I keep telling him that he must. A driving license is the most important ID in North America. It's the only proof of identity everyone asks for. If you ask me, it's more important than a health card or social insurance card."

"Why doesn't he apply for it then?" I said. "Is it because it's difficult to get one? I heard the inspectors make it really difficult to pass."

"That's true. I had to take the drive test thrice. Even Praful had to take the test twice. But in the case of Kumar, I think he's a little nervous about driving on the right side of the road. In India he was used to driving on the left hand side. I believe he gets all confused even while crossing the roads."

"Poor fellow," Naveen said.

* * *

Naveen was planning to shift base to Oshawa. As for myself, I neither went in for a rented basement apartment nor bought a house (semi-detached or otherwise), but found myself a comfortable but inexpensive room with shared toilet not too far away from Square One mall, the nerve centre of Mississauga.

The Prince too got the job he had applied for at Maple Plastics. He didn't look ecstatic, however.

"They're paying me the minimum wage. But they promised to increase my salary after the probation period."

"That's great," I said, though from what I heard I wasn't sure he would outlast his probation.

When he saw us prepare to leave, I think The Prince was sorely tempted to follow suit. He made enquiries about rents and bus routes. But nothing came out of it—he couldn't make up his mind, I guess.

I could never understand him. More than six months had passed since he came, but other than acquiring an enormous fund of Canadian lore, he had achieved nothing. Despite his braggadocio, he was deep down a funk—the reason, I presumed, for his pathological indecisiveness. He had dithered so long that he was too petrified now to leave the familiar environs of Chez Patel, and venture alone into the wide, open spaces of Canada.

A couple of months after I moved out, Falguni telephoned me: "Kumar's desperate. His bank balance is almost zero. He needs a job ASAP."

Without thinking twice, partly to oblige Falguni who is always helping others, partly to bail out a fellow Indian, I spoke to my manager. It was not difficult for him to set up an interview for The Prince as there was a lot of employee turnover in the telemarketing industry. He was so impressed with The Prince who could speak English well and even fetch up a Yankee accent at will (thanks to all the Westerns he saw in India) that he offered him a job right away.

The Prince came to work for two days, sold nary a directory, and disappeared without saying so much as a good bye.

I was furious, though I knew I had no one to blame but myself, and I had cut such a sorry figure before my boss. I gave Falguni a call.

"My apologies," she said. "He found telemarketing stressful, poor man. Besides, he's considering returning to India. His old employer is thinking of taking him back."

That came as no surprise. "Good for him," I said, but wasn't sure it was good for his *old* employer (whose hair The Prince would make even more grey)

A few days later, on my way to work as usual I bought a double-double, grabbed a free copy of Metro, and got into the subway car. I took a seat and started thumbing through the paper when I saw a news item that made my spine stiffen. "Road Accident in Mississauga: Yesterday, at a busy intersection near Square One, a 42-year-old pedestrian named Yuvraj Kumar was knocked down by a speeding car ...'

When I reached my office, the first thing I did was to call Falguni.

"Fortunately, Kumar's out of danger. But he is badly injured."

"What happened?"

"You know how the direction of traffic in Canada flusters him—he stepped on to the road without looking to his left. He moved one way then and then another, confusing the poor driver into hitting him."

My heart bled for the addled piece of mess we called The Prince. If ever there was a loser, it was him.

"Such a pity he's still single," Falguni said. "Had he been married, his wife would have looked after him."

"It's not too late. Finding a bride in India isn't hard."

"I know. He's not bad looking, he is well-educated, and his parents are well off. I wonder why he didn't get hooked?"

I could picture him seated in a marriage-broker's office, looking at one photograph after another of prospective brides, unable to decide on any, like the proverbial Buridan's ass. I told Falguni as much.

"What is a Buridan's arse?" she asked.

"*Ass*," I said. "He's a person who sits on his butt all day not wanting to take decisive action. The ass in the tale, unable to decide on which of the two baskets of straw to start with, dies of starvation." No sooner I said that than I bit my tongue.

"*Ram, Ram!*" Falguni said, invoking the gods.

"I'm sorry," I said. "Kumar will recover soon, I'm sure."

* * *

A few weeks later, when The Prince was on the way to recovery, I visited him at the Trillium. Reclining on a truckle bed, he looked cheerful.

"Hi," I said. "How are you feeling?"

"Not too bad," he said, eyeing the good looking blonde nurse who was jotting down something on a clipboard.

"How long are you required to stay in the hospital?"

Just then a dark-haired attendant entered the room. She proceeded to adjust his bed.

"Forever, I hope," he said, looking—in fact salivating—at the two nurses.

When the blond nurse left the room, he said: "So how's your telemarketing job?"

"Very stressful," I said drily.

"Sorry, *yaar*," he said, using the Hindi word for buddy. "I left your firm without giving notice. The commute took so much time and effort to reach downtown—taking a bus, a subway train and a streetcar. I don't know how you can do it twice every day."

"Don't bother about me," I said. "I heard you've convinced your old firm in India to take you back?"

He pointed to the side-table which had two envelopes on it. One of them, by the look of the blotchy postmark, must have surely originated in India. He said: "That's the offer letter. Now I can go back to India ... if I want to."

"Haven't you made up your mind?" I said, sighing.

He picked up the other letter and waved it at me.

"Do you know what this is?"

I shook my head. He told me that it was a letter from an ambulance-chaser outlining how to press for damages.

"So what are you going to do?" I should have known better than to ask him that question.

"I haven't decided," he said.

That was the last I saw of The Prince.

* * *

One day, while I was tidying my room, my cell phone trilled, sounding the theme song from *Catch Me If You Can* which I had installed. As always I had trouble finding my mobile, but eventually located it under the comforter next to my pillow.

"How are you?" It was Naveen.

"Fine," I said. "What about yourself?"

"Good, good," he said.

"How's the job?" I asked.

"Not bad. Even if the pay is so-so the health benefits are good."

I could detect a suspicion of disappointment in his voice. I said: "So, what's the matter? Doesn't it have much to do with ball bearings?"

"Well, not exactly. They only use needle bearings."

"That's too bad!" Apparently, for the *cognoscenti* there is a difference between ball bearings and needle bearings.

"Any news of The Prince?" Naveen asked.

"When last I heard of him he hadn't yet decided whether to return to India or stay back in Canada."

"That's so typical of him," Naveen said. "By the way, I bought a car. I'll come over in the afternoon, if it's OK with you."

"That will be great," I said. "Shall we have dinner at Bombay Bhel?"

"Done. Let's stop by the guesthouse on our way."

Later in the afternoon, Naveen tuned up in a rather beat-up car.

"Looks definitely pre-owned," I said.

"No," he said with a laugh. "It's a Chevy Cavalier." He

added: "It's ten years old, but it moves and keeps the cold out. That's enough for me."

We went in his car to Patels' guesthouse, dropping by unannounced, as they do in India. Falguni was delighted to see us; Praful had gone to the airport to receive a guest.

There were other newly arrived immigrant guests occupying the house now. One of the guests was in the solarium hunched over the computer (raking Internet sites for jobs, I was sure) while another was on the telephone (networking, no doubt). Somehow it was unsettling to see the johnnies-come-lately take over a place I had come to think of as home even if for a brief period of time. Kumar was nowhere in sight. It was unusual. You expected to find him hanging about like a household spirit, the mascot of the Patel guesthouse.

Falguni served us chai and No Name snacks.

"Where's Kumar?" Naveen said, picking up the mug of tea. "Has he gone with Praful to the airport?"

There was a silence, an awkward pause like when a social gaffe is committed.

"Is he all right?" Naveen asked, concerned.

"He has moved to the USA," Falguni said.

"How come?" I said. "Has he found a job there?"

"He received a large sum as compensation for his accident. He went on holiday to Florida and decided to settle down there."

"Wow!" Naveen said.

"Falguni, what do you mean by 'settled down'?" I said. "Has he got married or something?"

"Not exactly," she said, averting her gaze.

"I don't understand," I said. "What's Kumar up to?"

"What can I say?" said Falguni said. Reluctantly, her face pink with embarrassment, she revealed that Kumar had set up a *ménage a trois* in Tampa, with a blonde *and* a brunette.

Naveen's jaw dropped; I guffawed. The Prince had at last found a remedy for his chronic indecisiveness.

Weather Permitting

Ravi stood outside Mrs. Patel's guesthouse, shivering in an elegant but inadequate leather coat he had bought at a shop on Commercial Road in Bangalore. He was waiting for a taxi. A collection of voluminous bags and suitcases surrounded him like a rampart, as if providing a small measure of protection in an alien land.

Ravi was a slim, round-shouldered man in his mid-twenties. The slight stoop he had was the result of hunching over computer keyboards for long hours. He wore, as though dressed for the part, a pair of thick glasses. Even as he stood outside braving the autumnal weather, he removed his spectacles and wiped the lenses over and over again with his cloth handkerchief.

It was late fall—the trees were already looking gaunt and forlorn, and Ravi, newly arrived from India, was beginning to feel the cold. Routed by the near zero temperature, he bolted back into the lobby of Mrs. Patel's house. The spring door slammed shut behind him: it was only marginally warmer there, but he felt as if he had returned to a safe haven.

The front door opened suddenly, and Ravi found Mrs. Patel standing in the doorway.

"Hasn't your taxi come still?" she asked.

"No," said Ravi.

"It should be here anytime now," she said. "It is only five minutes since we called."

Even as they were talking, the taxi, whose overhead signage made it look like a police car, drew up in front of the house.

"Goodbye and good luck to you," Mrs. Patel said. "Let us know if you need any help."

The taxi driver, who looked South Asian, helped him to load the heavy suitcases into the trunk.

"What do they contain?" he asked. "Bricks?"

Yes, said Ravi to himself. *Of gold.*

"Only books," he said.

Ravi slid into the back, and gave the address to the driver.

"Are you new to Canada?" the driver asked, with the perceptiveness typical of a person in his profession.

"Yes. I landed about a month ago."

"Did you find a job? Or are you looking for one?"

"I got a job in a grocery store—just a temporary one until I can find one in my field."

"Is it the shop on the way to your house?"

"Yes," Ravi said.

"They don't pay well at a grocery store, do they?"

"I suppose not. But on weekends, they pay more."

"Lucky you! What was your profession back home?"

"I'm a software developer."

"The computer industry is down right now, I heard."

"I'm beginning to realise that," Ravi said, with a wry laugh.

When the taxi trundled up the last lonely stretch, the driver said: "This place is a little out of the way."

"Yes, as you can see it's not very far from my workplace. I was lucky to get the room."

"Really?"

The driver, having found the right street number, stopped in front of a rundown dwelling. The patch of grass in front of the house was unkempt, and weeds sprouted from the cracks in the path that lead to the front door. Ravi stepped out of the taxi. There was nobody about on the street. Except for a car parked on one of the driveways, the half dozen houses on the street looked eerily empty. The taxi driver helped Ravi disinter the suitcases from the trunk, and together they placed them at the front door.

Ravi paid the taxi driver, saying grandly: "Keep the change."

"You take care," the driver said. He had meant it as polite parting words, but for Ravi standing on the desolate curbside they had a chilling ring to them.

With its monotonous brown façade, his landlady's house looked no different from its neighbours except that it was more ramshackle than the rest. Ravi climbed the short flight of stairs that led to the front door and rang the bell. He waited for a few minutes and then rang the bell again. He heard the toccata of his landlady's walking stick even before the door was opened. Maya was a thin, tall woman with an untidy mass of silver and brown hair. Try as he might, Ravi could not place her nationality. One thing for sure, she was not a native Canadian. Going by her first name

she might even have come from India. Or at least of Indian
origin even she was from East Africa or the Caribbean, and
it could make her more sympathetic towards a new immigrant from India. From the tales he heard of the struggles
of new immigrants from the guys in the guest house, particularly Kumar, he could do with any help he got.

*But just look at the colour of her eyes! There's very little
chance that she could be from India.*

"I heard the bell the first time," she remarked, a tad
grumpily. Her two dogs were standing behind their mistress, peering at him with avid curiosity.

"I'm sorry," Ravi said.

Maya had a tiny frown on her brow, which Ravi was
soon to learn was a permanent feature. With an effort she
overcame the frown and managed to squeeze out a small
smile, like the last dregs of toothpaste. "Welcome," she said
as an afterthought. "Let me take you to your room."

She waited in silence, as if on sufferance, as Ravi moved
his enormous suitcases to the foot of the staircase.

"I'll take the luggage up later," he said.

"OK," she yielded grudgingly.

The solemn procession moved up the staircase slowly,
Maya's walking stick leading the way like some Roman
standard. Midway, the dogs broke away from the formation
like mutinous troops and raced up the staircase, barking
ecstatically. They sat down on the landing and stared at the
laggards, their tongues hanging out.

*I don't know why, but they remind me of the hounds from
Hell.*

Maya opened the door of a room and went inside. Ravi
followed her. The room, which Ravi had already seen once

before, was clean but had a rundown look like the rest of the house.

"Please keep the room neat and tidy," Maya said, thrusting two brass keys into his palm. "One key is for your room and the other for the front door. Don't lose them. If you do, you'll have to pay for the locks."

"Yes," Ravi said.

"I'll take you to the kitchen," Maya said.

She descended the staircase haltingly while an impatient Ravi shuffled behind her, keeping time to the thumping of the walking stick. The dogs tagged along, yelping all the while.

'Tough!" Maya said.

"Yes," Ravi said.

"I'm speaking to my dog."

"Rough!" Ravi said, recollecting the name of the dog.

"What?!" Maya said, looking suspiciously at him.

"I'm speaking to your dog."

They all arrived at the kitchen like a party of sightseers. Maya went up to the enormous fridge and opened its door. "This shelf is for you," she said. "Come, have a look."

Ravi walked up dutifully and peeped inside. While the rest of the fridge was occupied with bowls, boxes and bottles, one shelf was bare.

Next, Maya opened the freezer door and said: "This corner is for you."

Ravi looked over Maya's shoulder and saw swathes of meat wrapped in cellophane. He nodded dumbly. Ravi was a vegetarian; back home in India, his mother only used their fridge's tiny freezer to make ice and ice cream.

"This is the stove," Maya said, like a guide at a historical

site. Ravi looked at the gigantic cooking range. It had a bewildering array of knobs. "And this is the microwave, and
this is the toaster. You can use them, but mind you'll have
to pay if you break them."

"OK," Ravi said.

"Now I'll show you the laundry room."

She led him into the basement. The two dogs overtook
them and, joyously barking, threw themselves down the
staircase.

Maya opened the door of a room and switched on the
light. The room seemed to be full of jetsam from the ship
of Time: disused appliances, broken chandeliers, old magazines, and what have you. Marooned in a sea of orphaned
objects stood two large white cubes, tweedlewasher and
tweedledryer—once again with bewildering arrays of knobs
and buttons.

"I don't know how to use these things," Ravi said.
"You'll have to show me how."

"When you want to use them let me know and I'll show
you. Don't they have washing machines in Pakistan?"

"I wouldn't know."

"What about dryers?"

Ravi cast a glance at the humungous dryer.

*Everything in North America is enormous. The buildings,
the trucks, the cars ...*

"Back home in India we use a very, very big dryer," Ravi
said. "We call it the sun."

* * *

From the very moment he landed in Canada, Ravi wanted
to start looking for a job. But the other guys at Patel's guest-

house, having arrived before Ravi, showed him the right way of doing things. They told him about the Social Insurance Number card and how to acquire it. Without this piece of plastic you could not hope to land a job.

I suppose I'll have to wait for my SIN card to catch up with me

There were other cards too, a whole deck of them, in fact: health card, credit card, debit card, permanent residence card and the ultimate trump card—the driver's license. Whether you drove or not, it was advisable to get yourself one; in North America precious little could be done without it.

And I must be the joker in the pack! Back home, I didn't even have a business card, let alone a credit card or a debit card.

When he visited a government office-cum-information centre to apply for his SIN card, he stumbled upon what he thought was a goldmine of information. There were booklets galore overflowing out of large wooden racks. Rows and rows of PC's beckoned you to come over and start your job search at once. Voluminous directories sat on the shelves bursting with names, addresses, telephone numbers and website details of companies in Canada, incorporated or otherwise.

With such resources at hand, even the most incorrigible pessimist could be forgiven for thinking that finding job in Canada was a piece of cake. But, nothing, nothing prepared Ravi for the horrendous reality. He sent out countless CV's by email and fax, but not one response did he get.

"If you think getting a job is that easy," Kumar—aka "The Prince" as some of the residents called him—had said, "you're living in a fool's paradise."

Kumar, who unlike most of the other residents had been living in the Patel guesthouse for many months, came across as worldly-wise and, whether petitioned or not, went about freely dispensing advice.

"First of all, you will have to start calling your CV a *resume*," Kumar said. "And write it the way they do in Canada. Don't include details like marital status or hobbies. There are books available in local libraries which will help you in making a resume."

Ravi wrestled with a big, fat DIY book on resumes for two days, and produced one which seemingly conformed to the way resumes are composed in Canada. He sent it out by email and fax to software companies whose names he had culled from business directories. But all he got in return was a stony silence. He attended classes conducted by the YMCA on resume-writing. He re-engineered his resume and sent it out once again over web and wire. He was seriously thinking of changing his name to Ryan or Raymond to improve his chances, when he did get a reply. The email was very polite and short. It thanked him for his interest, but regretted that the position was already filled from within. He would have laughed out loud had it not been so Kafkaesque.

You have to be within to get in. What kind of hellish paradox is this?

Taking the public transit, he visited every software company whose address he could lay his hands on—he was directed to leave his resume at the reception, or sometimes even with the security guard. His paper trail took him to almost every nook and corner of Toronto—downtown, the Metro area, and the GTA. This way he learnt so much about the city that he even nursed the idea of becoming a taxi-driver or a bus-driver until Kumar The Prince shot it down.

"Let me tell you something. It's easier to become the Governor-General of Canada than landing either of these jobs."

Ravi felt so helpless that he wanted to cut and run.

Is this the better life I was looking for? Is it for this that I paid thousands of Rupees to the immigration consultant in India?

But one providential day, on his way back from a job-fair, he met a fellow Indian on a bus. They started a polite conversation. It turned out that the stranger, whose name was Ghulam Hussain, hailed from Hyderabad too. He told him of a grocery shop where he had worked for while. He gave Ravi the name of the manager, and said: "Why don't go and meet him?"

"Will he give me a job?" Ravi asked. "Just like that?"

"Why not give it a try?" Hussain said. "There's no guar-antee, but I know the manager well. Give my name as reference."

Ravi got off the bus and went straight to the grocery store. He met the manager. And when he got the job, he could not believe his luck.

A low-paying job, no doubt. But what mattered most was that he had one!

"Way to go," Mrs. Patel said. "Now, you can hunt for your software job at your leisure. P'raps, you can even get yourself a Canadian certification of some kind in your field. It will help you."

"Be careful," Kumar had warned. "If I were you, I wouldn't rush off to get myself any certificate. There are many insti-tutes here that are ready to hand out certificates. Let me tell you, these certificates are not worth the paper they are printed on."

Now that he had a job in hand, Ravi started looking for a place to stay. Mr. Patel gave him the telephone numbers of their erstwhile guests who had apparently made it in Canada. Some of them had prospered enough to have bought houses and were letting out the basement to help them pay off the mortgage. He called and spoke to them. Either there was no room or the place was too far away from his store.

Ravi bought a copy of the *Mississauga News* and went through the classifieds. He short-listed the houses that were in the vicinity of his store. He rang up the landlords one by one to make appointments. One landlord seemed to lose his enthusiasm the moment he heard Ravi's accent, and said that the room was already let out. Often Ravi had to leave messages on answering machines. But two of the landlords called back and invited him to check the place out for himself.

The first house he visited turned out to be in a well-heeled neighbourhood which sported large detached houses with shady trees and well-kept lawns. The landlord was a Pakistani and the house reeked of *biryani*. The room was airy and looked over a lovely creek, but was way too expensive and the landlord wouldn't climb down on the rent.

The next house belonged to Maya. But the *de facto* owners seemed to be her two dogs: one named Ruff and the other named Tuff. As Maya quizzed Ravi, her dogs looked on gravely as if they were judges at a game show. All through the interview, Maya wore a smile which seemed forced, as if it were something she had applied to her lips like lipstick, and was going to wipe it away with Kleenex the moment the meeting was over.

The house was tolerably clean but had that fallen-on-hard-times look. The bedroom window gave on to a deso-late farm which showed no signs of life. A disused railway line separated the neighbourhood from the main part of the city. Even then it wasn't too bad. He had heard of new immigrants being cooped up in basement-bedrooms with-out a single window. What's more, Maya was amenable to negotiation. They arrived at a mutually agreed price and Ravi sealed the deal with a token advance.

As she took his hundred-dollar bill, Maya said: "Re-member, you will have to pay first and last."

"Yes," Ravi said. Kumar had primed him well. He had explained, without ever being asked to, what the puzzling clause in the classifieds meant. A tenant had to pay two months' rent when he moved in. And when he moved out the landlord would return one month's rent like a parting gift, provided the tenant had not broken the bathtub or set the kitchen on fire.

It's another way of taking rent in advance; anyway it was better than the three months' rent the landlords in India de-manded in advance. Landlords are the same everywhere!

* * *

On Monday morning, Ravi woke up even before the alarm rang. He had a shower and got into his uniform. He went into the kitchen and made himself a cup of coffee and a sandwich. After finishing his breakfast he washed the plate and the mug and replaced it in the cabinet. He wiped the dining table with care so that his landlady, who seemed to have a mania for cleanliness, would have no cause for complaint.

Outside, the wind was blowing, and it felt very cold. Yet, Ravi decided against taking the bus: public local transit wasn't cheap in this country. After he had been walking for a few minutes, he could feel the cold invade his body; the wind that came sweeping down from the North Pole made short shrift of his skimpy leather coat. And the gloves he had picked up in a dollar store were no match either. He shivered, and began to walk faster, stuffing his fists into his pockets.

When he arrived at the store, he bolted inside as though he was being pursued by a predator. The supervisor who answered to the name of Zack was on his way to the cold room, briskly pushing an empty trolley. He was a lanky, tousle-haired kid who was just out of school. He also looked, for good measure, as if he was just out of bed. Somehow, it did not seem right to Ravi that a chit of a guy like Zack should put him through his paces.

"The apples are low we have to refill them. Let's go to the back of the store. I'll show you how to do it."

Zack and Ravi loaded the big white boxes containing apples on to a dolly and wheeled them to the front of the shop. Zack showed Ravi how to arrange fresh apples on the counter—Ravi never imagined that there was a well thought out strategy behind such a quotidian task.

"The fresh apples must go to the back and bottom," Zack explained. "This is called 'rotating'."

Quickly and expertly he moved the old apples on to the dolly and replenished the counter with fresh ones. Later, he poured the old ones on top, within easy reach of the customers.

How I wish I could work some magic like this with my resume —somehow make it more attractive to the potential employers.

"While you're at it, you must pick out damaged or rotting fruit," Zack said, tossing a damaged apple into a box.

Zack also showed him how to arrange the 'drop', a counter-high pile of boxes in the front with the topmost box open, showing up the fruit. This made the table look bursting and full, a merchandiser's vision of cornucopia.

North America is a land of plenty. One day in future I hope I'll also be able to shop until I drop, and not keep counting pennies like I'm doing now.

Once he learnt the drill, Ravi did oranges on his own. And then he had to do carrots, then potatoes, and then lemons and so on and so forth—stopping only for breaks: one for lunch that was unpaid and two others of 15-minute duration which were paid.

If I have to do this day after day, I'll surely go bananas.

By the end of the day, Ravi's body was sore as hell. Nonetheless, Ravi derived a modicum of satisfaction from the fact that he had done what was undeniably hard labour and still managed to get through the day. In the bargain, he made some money, too. He swiped his ID card and started for home, exhausted but exhilarated.

* * *

As he neared Maya's house, Ravi was surprised to see a dusty old Ford noisily back out of the driveway. He glimpsed a shadowy form at the wheel as the car zipped past him.

Ravi fumbled for the keys in his pocket with his frozen, insensitive fingers. When he opened the door and stepped in, he found that the light was turned on in the kitchen. Maya came out as he was getting out of his shoes.

"Good evening," he said.

"Good evening." Her smile had gone AWOL.

"Would you be able to show me how to use the washing machine? I'd like to wash my clothes in the evening."

"Not today," Maya said, with unmerited brusqueness. "You must wash your clothes only on weekends."

"All right," Ravi said—and went up to his room.

Having nothing better to do, he put on the TV. He had picked it up dirt cheap at a clearance outlet. The guys in the guesthouse had told him that it was always good to have a TV as it gave the weather forecast, which was so vital in Canada.

He surfed the channels but found nothing to hold his attention, so he shut the TV off and decided to write the long overdue letter to his mother. His father had died when he was seven. His mother had borrowed money from her brothers so that Ravi could show proof of funds to the Canadian High Commission. With carefully chosen words he informed her that he had started working, glossing over the fact that the apples and the McIntoshes he handled had nothing to do with computers.

After he finished writing the letter, he walked over to the window and looked out. It was getting dark already and the desolate landscape, as if painted only in shades of black and grey, looked bleak and unreal, like something out of a sci-fi movie. He was seized by an unaccountable feeling of emptiness. Though the feeling was not one of hunger, he went into the kitchen and cooked himself a simple meal of boiled rice and vegetable curry. As he was eating, he heard Maya's walking stick thudding hollowly on the carpeted stairs as she made her way up from the basement. Ruff and Tuff shot out like cannon balls, even before Maya emerged.

When she came into the kitchen, she looked around intently. She examined the cooking range and the microwave. She picked up a kitchen cloth and ran it over the countertop, though Ravi had already wiped it down thoroughly.

She looks as if she's spoiling for a fight.

And then without uttering a single word Maya limped out of the room. The dogs, as if sensing their mistress's mood, followed her solemnly like good-conduct-medal winning sheep. After finishing his meal, Ravi went back to his room feeling a little uncomfortable.

* * *

Ravi was utterly disappointed when he read the weekly work schedule that was tacked to the wall in the staff room. He found that he got to work for only three days a week. In his naiveté he had expected to get a full five-day, 40-hour week. Three days meant just 24 hours of work. After paying his grocery bills, there would be hardly anything left. He needed to buy clothes for the fast-approaching winter.

On this piddling salary I can't afford anything! I'll never be able to buy even a jalopy, let alone a Mustang I've always dreamed of.

Zack had formed the opinion that Ravi was slow. In spite of working like a fiend, he was unable to alter Zack's assessment. Once Zack made up his mind, that was that. He wasn't going to change it any time soon. Neither was he going to offer Ravi more hours nor increase his salary. It was better for Ravi to look for another job.

So it's back to square one now!

On the days he was free, he began to visit the Y again. There he surfed the web, and sent out his resumes. He started going to the public library again and sifted through the newspapers looking for suitable positions. He began to attend job-fairs no matter which part of Toronto they were held in.

Not one month had passed since he had landed his job, and the initial euphoria had all but evaporated.

* * *

Ravi was on his way to the Y one afternoon when he ran into a neighbour. The man was tinkering with his car, an older model BMW. As Ravi walked past him, the man smiled and said: "Hi! How you're doing?"

It had been a long time since he saw a smile on someone's face. Maya had irretrievably misplaced hers, and Zack apparently reserved his exclusively for speed demons.

"I'm fine. How about you?" Ravi said, trembling in the cold.

"Good, good," the man said. "Is it already too cold for you? Where are you from? India?"

"Yes. Are you from India too?"

"I'm from Trinidad. My name's Tony. The cold bothers me too. Anyways, I'm going home for vacation. I won't be back until after the New Year."

"Lucky you."

"You should take a break too. Go somewhere warm."

"Unfortunately, I'm stuck here for the winter—I can't afford a vacation right now."

"That's too bad," Tony said, pulling the hood down. "Maybe next year."

"I hope so."

"It was nice talking to you," Tony said, before going back into his house.

In the last few weeks this brief snatch of conversation was the only friendly, ordinary, human exchange he had had. The place he lived and the place he worked both made him feel small and of little account.

* * *

He entered the house and was getting out of his shoes, when he heard the sickening tock-tock of Maya's walking stick. There was a feeling of inevitableness associated with the sound—as if something unpleasant were sure to follow. He knew this feeling would dog him always—unless he found a means of escape.

The three conspirators came out of the kitchen. Maya said: "Ray-vee, I want to speak to you." The dogs standing on either side of Maya and staring steadfastly at him seemed to second her wish.

"Yes?" said Ravi, inwardly squirming.

"Remember to wipe your shoes on the mat outside," she said tetchily, sidetracked for a moment.

"OK, I'm sorry," Ravi said. He added hopefully: "Is that all?"

"No! I found breadcrumbs all over the kitchen counter. Why don't you clean up after you use the kitchen?"

"I only had a cup of coffee in the morning."

"Then where did the breadcrumbs come from?"

"How am I to know?"

"Nobody lives here other than you and me!"

"I've already told you—" Ravi stopped short. He didn't

want to start a fight. He was a peaceable man, though there was many a time in his life when he wished he had shown some pluck rather than give in easily. But he had not come to Canada to fight every step of his way. He added tamely: "OK, I'll be careful, next time."

Ravi went up to his room. Though he felt like having a snack he did not want to go downstairs again. He put on the TV and watched it inattentively. The weather details were being continuously shown in a corner of the screen. How important weather was in this country! In India nobody bothered so much about it. The weatherman was only remembered at the end of summer when people waited for the onset of monsoon to cool the parched earth.

He switched off the TV, and picked up the John Grisham he had borrowed from the library. He read for a long time, totally absorbed, until he heard Maya pottering about in the kitchen downstairs. The French windows juddered as they were dragged open by Maya. Ruff and Tuff barked joyously.

She's letting the dogs out for exercise. It's a wonder they don't freeze to death.

As he continued to read the book, he thought he heard someone knocking on a door on the ground floor. He ignored it—who would be doing that? After some time he heard the doorbell ring. It rang urgently, persistently. Maya always took time to answer the doorbell, what with her limp and her walking stick. To say nothing of her dogs weaving around her legs and slowing her down even more. But who would visit her so late in the night? Nobody ever came to the house except Maya's prospective tenants answering her ads. (She had a vacant room next to his for which there were no takers. They gave her decaying house a quick once-over and never came back.)

Perhaps, it's her son.

Ravi had never met Maya's son in the flesh. He had learned much later that the figure he had seen driving the Ford was her son. In her conversations with Ravi, Maya referred to her son as her boy. An almost mythical figure, Ravi was made aware of the son's existence only by the mood swings he caused in his hapless mother.

Then he heard the front door being pounded rather than knocked. Though it was not his call, he got up from his bed and crept down the stairs. The light was on in the kitchen, yet the house seemed deserted. Nonetheless he half-expected to hear the tock-tock of Maya's stick—she might hobble out of a room anytime and give him a cold, disapproving look—as was her wont nowadays.

What has become of the loathsome threesome?

He opened the front door cautiously. He was startled to see Maya on the other side. She looked rattled but her relief on seeing him was obvious. The dogs insinuated themselves into the house, even before he could open the door to its full extent.

"Thank you," Maya said, shivering. She seemed to be wearing only a housecoat. "I took the dogs into the yard for exercise and would have been out only for a few minutes. But the French-windows got locked behind me. There's something wrong with the catch. I should tell my son to fix it."

Maya gave him a watery smile and said: "Good night, Ray-vee."

* * *

The first snow came in the middle of November when it was not yet officially winter. Ravi stood at his window and watched it falling. At first, it fell like a light rain of petals in Indian mythological films. The brown and green earth was gradually drained of its colour. Soon, the world was nothing but a roiling mass of spinning snowflakes—it was as if a billowing white curtain had been drawn across the window.

He had been waiting with dread for the first snow to fall, the weather was bad enough as it was. He pulled the blinds shut and lay down on his bed. He switched on the TV and tried to watch an ongoing English movie. It failed to lift his spirits.

After a couple of hours, it stopped snowing. Reluctantly, Ravi decided to go out and see how it felt. Wearing the heavy out-of-fashion coat, boots, and gloves he had bought at a discount outlet, he felt like a medieval knight in full armour. Locking the door behind, he gingerly stepped into a landscape covered with snow for the first time in his life. The road, the sidewalk and the lawn he had seen day in and day out had disappeared as though erased with whiteout.

It was afternoon, and the scene outside could easily have decorated a Christmas card. The snow dripped like icing from rooftops. Wisps of snow hung from trees. A wan sun began to shine, and the air had acquired a crisp, crystalline quality. To his surprise, Ravi discovered that it was not as cold as he had feared. He plodded through the virginal snow, leaving a trail of deep, dark scars behind him. In the ankle-deep snow, it was hard to make out where the sidewalk ended and where the road began. When he reached a busy intersection, he noticed the traffic had slowed down as the driving conditions had worsened because of the weather. Just a few yards from where Ravi was standing, all of a sudden, a speeding car lost control on the snow smeared road and slalomed into another with a thunderous crash, like they did in Hollywood action movies. Unused to seeing such sights back home, the accident put a fright into Ravi. He had no idea how dangerous roads could become in the winter. He made a quick about turn and scurried back home.

* * *

Christmas was almost upon them, and at the store there was expectation in the air. Thanks to the holiday rush, the staff would get more hours of work. This meant more pay. But in Ravi's case no such thing happened. He continued to get his usual, measly quota of 24 hours.

I'll surely get the heave ho after the holiday season. I must do something soon.

When Zack walked past Ravi on one of his rounds, Ravi stopped him.

"Zack, I want to speak to you."

"What is it?" Zack said, with the usual smirk on his face.

"Is there any way I can get more hours? The money I make is not enough for me to live on. "

"Ravi, you should be happy with the hours you are getting. The store is given only so many hours by our home office. We divvy up the hours among all the employees as best as we can."

"Others are getting much more than me. I work just as hard as them."

"You're a bit slow, so your productivity is low."

"I'm not used to this kind of work, yet I do it with sincerity. I'm always trying to do my best."

"Your best, Ravi," said Zack, as though choosing his words carefully, "is not good enough."

Zack may as well have shot a bullet into Ravi's heart. Ravi was too stunned to reply. If his circumstances were different, he would have quit his job then and there.

As an immigrant one must learn to not just eat but feast on humble pie.

However upset he was, there was little he could do. Things were bad in the IT sector right then. How many times can you send out your resumes? How many times can you make cold calls? How many times can you visit job-fairs?

One week before Christmas, returning from work, he walked right into an ambush. As he shut the front door behind him, he heard the portentous tock-tock before Maya before into the room. Ruff and Tuff came in her wake but were subdued but watchful.

What now?

"Hi," said Ravi. "A very cold day, eh?"

"Er ... Hi," she said, caught off guard. Then she added, recovering her usual bad temper: "What have you done to the washing machine?"

"Nothing," Ravi said. "I used it the day before yesterday. It was working fine."

"It's broken, now. You were the last person to use it. Do you know how much it costs to fix that damn thing?"

Ravi was, as usual, at a loss for words.

"You were the last person to use it and you must pay—" Maya started to say, working herself into a rage.

"Can I take a look at it? I may be able to fix it."

"How can you fix it? You had never used a washing machine in your life before!"

"Maybe your son can repair it?" Ravi said.

"My son! That good for nothing boy. He only comes here to gouge money out of me. And eat my food."

"Mine, too" said Ravi.

"What?! What did you say?"

"I said he takes my food from the refrigerator," Ravi said slowly, as if talking to a half-deaf person.

"My son ... he's ... he's not a thief," Maya said loudly. But she didn't look very convinced herself.

"Somebody is helping himself to my food. There are only two of us here."

"How dare you talk to me like that? If you don't like it here, you may leave."

"I would, if it was not the middle of winter!"

"Who cares? You must look for another house immediately." Maya was almost screaming now.

"OK," said Ravi. "I'll do that."

Enough's enough.

"Until the machine is repaired you will have to use the coin laundry. Do you understand?"

"I don't have a car. How do expect me to go to a coin laundry in this weather?"

"That's not my problem."

Ravi went up to his room, cursing himself for needlessly precipitating the matter. Yet, he was glad that he had spoken up. At every turn nowadays he was finding himself at the receiving end.

But the thought of the additional expense disheartened him. Not only had he to pay for the laundry, he needed take a bus to get to the nearest Laundromat.

I can't take things lying down anymore. I'm literally being taken to the cleaners!

He went up to his room and put on the music system

he had bought at a yard sale. A vigorous Bollywood tune gushed out, and Ravi turned up the volume. He lay down on the bed without changing out of his work clothes, trying not to think. The music failed to lift his spirits, but it reminded him of home.

No! I'm not going back ... I'm not going to give up.

He scrambled out of his bed, rooted out his small address book, and looked under 'S'. Shyam owned a town house and was letting out his basement. Ravi had spoken to him when he was looking for a room the first time.

"Hi, I'm Ravi," he said into the mouth piece, lowering the stereo volume with the remote. "I called you two months ago. Do you remember?"

"I do," Shyam said. "You're from Hyderabad, aren't you?"

"Yes. You wanted me to give you a call in the last week of December."

"I'm sorry, Ravi. The basement is not vacant. My tenant was supposed to move out, but he has changed his mind."

Ravi put down the phone. Absentmindedly, he pulled out his glasses and began polishing the lenses. Then he lunged for the phone and called Mrs. Patel. Once the pleasantries were over he asked if she would have a travel agent's phone number. "Is everything all right back home?"

"Everything's fine. I want to go on holiday."

"They must be paying you well at the grocery shop! Give me a moment. I'll look for the number."

Once he got the number, Ravi rang the travel agent. He was put on hold for a good 15 minutes before the agent came on line.

"Can you book me on a flight to Hyderabad? Today ...Yes, it's an emergency ... in another 5 hours via New York?

That's perfect. No problem, I'll give you my credit card number ..."

Cranking up the volume again, Ravi began to pack all his things, stuffing his meagre wardrobe between stacks of books he never got to use. There was no place for his voluminous winter wear. He would have to leave it behind. This brought a shadow of a smile to his face—he was never ever going to see snow again in his life.

He peeled off his uniform, like he was sloughing off his outworn skin. He threw the dark green golf shirt with a yellow logo—his badge of shame—into the trash can. Suddenly, he felt liberated, and his mood began to improve somewhat.

Then he heard the banging on his door.

It must be Maya. The Hindi film number must have drowned out the tock-tock of her cane. How nice!

Ravi opened the door. Framed by the doorway was a grim-faced Maya, her walking stick lending her magisterial look.

"Your music is too loud," she yelled over the *dhoom-thana dhoom-thana* of the Bollywood dance number.

"Sorry about that. I'll reduce the sound."

"Thank you, but don't let it happen again—I find it hard to climb the stairs."

"There will be no next time," Ravi said. "I'm vacating the house tonight."

Without a change in her expression, Maya said in an icy voice: "I can't return the last month's rent tonight."

"Keep it," Ravi said, as if to a waiter.

Her eyes—they are grey, Arctic grey. Like lumps of ice.

Maya turned away without saying another word.

Ravi shut off the music and put on the TV, taking care to keep the volume down. A weather alert was being announced. It was going to be the coldest night of the season. People were warned not to venture outdoors without protective gear. Actually, he would have liked nothing better than to step out of the house and get himself a coffee from the closest Tim Hortons, which was by no means close. But he knew how treacherous the ice covered sidewalks were. Returning home from work, he had to pick his way with care lest he slipped and fell. The snow on the ground had turned into ice—glassy and deadly.

Ravi continued to watch the program drained of all energy, the cost of the spat with Maya. In another two hours he would have to leave for the airport.

He was exhausted from the hard work he had put in at the grocery store, and a lethargic feeling stole over him. In spite of himself, he began to doze. As though in a dream he heard Ruff and Tuff bark with joy somewhere far away. He heard the peculiar pizzicato as the French-windows were pulled opened.

I wouldn't be out on a night like this. If I slipped and fell, there's nobody about to help me.

He slept fitfully, subconsciously aware that he had a plane to catch. Whenever he woke up and forced open his stinging eyes, he saw a noisy, incoherent spectacle being played out on the TV. But just as soon he drifted back into sleep. As he dozed he thought he heard the insistent ringing of a doorbell, but it sounded faint and remote.

Could it be Maya? Was she locked out again?

Who cares?

Sleep overpowered him again, and he slipped into blissful slumber, thinking that he would be soon on his way home.

An hour later he woke up with a start. He felt groggy and disoriented. He took some moments to realise that he had to leave for the airport. He looked at his watch. It was 9 pm. He had two hours. He could still make it if he hurried.

He switched off the TV, and looked out to the window. The night was still and lifeless under a pall of haze. But when he thought of home—a vision bathed in light—he cheered up no end. He would have to leave the TV and music system behind, his parting gifts for Maya. He called a cab and wheeled his suitcase out, locking the room behind him.

When he went downstairs, the house was quiet. The light in the kitchen was on, but there was the touch and feel of an unoccupied house. He went to the head of the stairs that lead to the basement and called out for Maya. There was no reply, no evidence of Ruff and Tuff either. He checked his impulse to go down and rouse them.

How furious Maya will be if I walked into her bedroom!

He recollected the vague sounds he had heard in his sleep. Was it a dream or had Maya got locked out once again?

I hope not. She may not have been on the best of terms with me ... but I wish her no harm. She must be fast asleep, that's all.

When he stepped out of the house, the cold air struck him like a physical blow. As he waited for his taxi trembling in his leather coat, he heard the ebb and flow of traffic on a nearby highway. He looked up and down the street—no other signs of life out there. In the distance, stray dogs barked.

Are there stray dogs in Canada?

He heard the piercing wail of a squad car somewhere on the main road. A car with a lighted signage on the roof appeared on the street. It was no police cruiser but only his taxi. Turning into Maya's driveway, it stopped in front of the house.

With a quizzical expression, the driver helped him load the heavy suitcase into the trunk.

"They are only books," Ravi said.

"You like reading, eh?" the driver said.

"Take me to Terminal One—I'm in a hurry," Ravi said, climbing into the cab.

The taxi backed out of the driveway and nosed its way to the main road, while the mist shifted like smoke around them. A few minutes later, a flashing ambulance, bellowing like a monster with laryngitis, overtook them. It stopped a few hundred metres up the road. There was already a squad car parked there, with its headlights burrowing into the darkness. As the taxi sped past the scene, Ravi saw the silhouettes of two dogs milling about.

"Some fool taking his dog for walk on a night like this must have slipped and fallen," the cab driver remarked.

Could it be Maya? Could the dogs be Ruff and Tuff? Should we stop and have a look? There's no time, if we do, I'll miss my flight.

The driver eased the taxi on to the ramp that led to the highway. As the taxi slipped seamlessly into the scant traffic, he said: "Weather permitting, you will be in time for your flight."

The Tamarind Relish

The moment Savitri saw the large snow-white envelope —even before her eyes fell on the shiny postage stamp that said "Canada"—she knew that it was from Satya.

Savitri wore a paper-stiff cotton sari and her hair was combed and plaited tightly. She looked pretty in a demure sort of way. She had been married to Satya for almost two years.

Savitri selected a silver-inlaid paperknife they had got as a wedding present and tore open the envelope with it. She pulled out a sheaf of official-looking forms along with a single sheet of notepaper. The latter was deckled at the top, where it had been wrenched from a pad.

Savitri picked up the letter and began to read:

Toronto,
16.6.05
Dear Savvy,
Hope this letter finds you in the best of health.

   I am enclosing the immigration forms for Amma.
Please help her fill them out. If you have any questions,

let me know. Regarding your visa and landing papers, you should hear from the High Commission any time now ...

"What has Satya written?" asked Chandramma, Savitri's mother-in-law. She was about 60 years old and a widow. She had blunt facial features with two large front teeth. Her greasy gray-black hair was tied into a shapeless bun at her nape.

Savitri looked up from the letter. "Satya has sent immigration forms for you to fill up, Amma," she said.

"I don't know if I want to go and live in Canada at my age. All the ice I see in the calendar Satya sent us! I don't think I can bear that kind of cold. Anyway, what else has he written?"

Savitri started to read aloud: "A friend of mine will be returning to India soon. Do you want anything from Canada? It shouldn't be something big (or expensive either). I'm sending the Ziploc bags which Amma wanted with him ..."

"So he has remembered!" Chandramma said. "I find those bags so convenient to use, and it's so hard to get them here."

Savitri resumed reading out from the letter: "That reminds me. I have requested Revant (he is an old friend and schoolmate of mine, you'd have met him at our wedding reception) to teach you how to use a computer so that you can send e-mails to me."

"Wouldn't they be expensive?" Chandramma said. "And we don't have a computer at home, either."

"They are far cheaper than a telephone call. I'll have to go to the PCO down the street to read his emails—you know, the small shop next to Janata Super Market which has a large sign that says 'ISD/STD'."

"I see. What else does Satya say?"

"When I returned to Canada," Savitri read, lending her voice to Satya's words, "my friends were very disappointed when they came to know I hadn't brought any of Amma's tamarind pickle. The pickle has become famous in Mississauga too! I think you should learn how to make it."

Chandramma's face glowed with pleasure and she twittered happily: "I just didn't find enough time to make the pickle when Satya was here last month. His trip was so sudden and short. And, you know, I don't like to make the pickle in a hurry-burry. I like to take a lot of care while preparing the tamarind pickle. One slip and it's sure to spoil."

Savitri had heard her mother-in-law say that so often in reference to the tamarind pickle—"one slip and it's sure to spoil", as though it was some ancient motto of Satya's family. Doubtless, Chandramma was proud of her skill in making a variety of pickles and condiments; and she generously distributed the stuff she made to her grateful friends and relatives.

Even Savitri had to admit that her mother-in-law's tamarind pickle was excellent as pickles went. Chandramma used to speak about the making of this particular pickle as if it were a sacred ritual. In Satya's family there were many rituals and, soon after her marriage, Savitri was given a crash course on them. When she entered the house for the very first time, kicking the tumbler of rice placed on the threshold, she was also kicking away her past life as if it were an ill-fitting shoe.

In the old days, a bride even had to change her first

name when she came to her husband's home. Anyway, her mother-in-law had liked the name "Savitri"; it was nice and reassuringly old-fashioned. Savitri's namesake in mythology was a steadfast and devoted wife who had outwitted Yama, the God of Death, into sparing her husband's life.

And Satya, in an uncharacteristic show of romance, had shortened her name to "Savvy". But truth to tell, Satya had reckoned that "Savvy" would be easy on Canadian tongues. When Savitri came to know of the real motive, she had felt a twinge of disappointment.

Even though two full years had not passed since her marriage, Savitri's past life already seemed so unreal and remote now—as though she was looking from the wrong end of a telescope. She had grown up in an industrial town in north India, where her father had worked in a steel plant. Savitri used to spend her evenings playing table-tennis at the company club or watching Bollywood films in an open air theatre.

But when her father's retirement loomed over their future, a manhunt was launched to find a suitable "match" for Savitri. Photographs and horoscopes flew back and forth before her marriage was finally "arranged". When her friends and class-mates came to know that her fiancé was a chemical engineer working in Canada, they could barely hide their envy. That Satya was working as a security guard at a pharmaceutical company was another matter. It was only a few months ago that he had found regular employment as a machine operator in the same factory.

Savitri was married off in a twinkle and, before she realised she was no more a virgin, she was honeymooning in Ooty. The breathless succession of betrothal, wedding and honeymoon made Savitri feel as if she was seated in a madly spinning merry-go-round.

Then suddenly the whirligig stopped. Satya left for Canada, leaving her behind in a dingy apartment in Hyderabad in south India, with only his widowed mother for company. Savitri had thought that her stay in Hyderabad would be a short stint in purgatory after which she would be led soon to the paradise that was Canada (with Chandramma, no doubt, playing the role of a fussy Beatrice). But the Canadian High Commission was taking its own sweet time in issuing Savitri her landing papers, so she was left to languish in her mother-in-law's house.

How indescribably boring life had become! Other than watching TV or listening to her mother-in-law's gossip about Satya's relatives, there was little else to do. She had no friends in Hyderabad, or relatives who could be called kindred spirits. The only people who would call on them were Amma's female acquaintances, with an average age of 50 plus or higher. As to going out, once a week the two would visit a temple close by... An alien life for a young woman who had spent most of her life in a company township, spending almost every evening with youthful friends of both sexes, playing sports, watching films, going out on picnics, hikes, and long drives.

When the telephone rang, Savitri had almost finished reading the letter. Chandramma, cheered up with news of Satya, shot up from her seat to answer the phone.

"Hello! Revant? How are you, son? I don't see you at all nowadays ... Yes, she was telling me that. She's here ... please talk to her." She handed over the receiver to Savitri.

"Hi, Savvy. How's life?" The voice, which Savitri found

attractive, had an urbane drawl that people who went to expensive schools acquired.

"Fine, thank you."

"Satya wanted me to show you how to use the Internet. Do you know how to use a PC?"

"No." She'd learn how to use a computer time and again, but not having the need to use one regularly it had always remained an enigma.

"Not computer-savvy, what?" Savitri thought she detected a hint of flirtation. The voice continued: "Not to worry. It is all so easy nowadays. You can learn it in a jiffy. I'm free tomorrow afternoon. What about you?"

"I'm free too," Savitri said, sighing inwardly—she had all the time in the world, but nothing much to do.

"Tomorrow at 4 o'clock then."

Savitri put down the phone. She said: "Amma, Satya's friend Revant is coming to pick me up tomorrow evening. He wants to show me how to use the computer."

"I've not seen Revant in ages! It's all right Savitri if he's coming in the evening. I'm planning to make the tamarind pickle tomorrow after lunch. You can learn how to make it."

"Where's the hurry, Amma? My going to Canada is still a long way off."

"Never mind, dear. It has been a long time since I've made the pickle. Mrs. Boothalingam asked me the other day when I would be making the pickle. We can send a couple of jars to your parents, too."

* * *

Chandramma had been feeling so restless in the aftermath of Satya's return to Canada that she jumped at the chance of doing something associated with her son. The very next day a chirpy and beaming Chandramma went to the market to buy the ingredients for the pickle. There she drove the shopkeepers crazy with her habit of continually grumbling about rising prices and falling quality while she scrutinized every item thoroughly. Chandramma returned home with a collection of carry bags in each hand, sweating profusely and complaining about the heat and dust.

After taking a bath, Chandramma went into the kitchen to make the pickle. She examined and cleaned all the ingredients one by one and arranged them on the kitchen counter. She ferreted out an ancient diary from a cupboard, and thrust it into Savitri's hands.

"Many of these recipes were given to me by my mother-in-law," she said. "Even the recipe for the tamarind pickle, for that matter. My mother-in-law used to say that one had to be pure in mind and body while making the tamarind pickle or else ..."

"... it would spoil," completed Savitri for her mother-in-law.

"You're right," Chandramma said.

Savitri took the diary and riffled the pages until she came across the recipe for the tamarind pickle. The page was smudged with oily, ochre-coloured finger marks, as if an avant-garde artist had provided the illustrations for her mother-in-law's text.

Savitri placed the diary on the kitchen counter, and then went and stood next to her mother-in-law. Chandramma, wearing the apron Satya had brought for her from Canada, presided over an enormous, sputtering pan. Savitri handed out ladles, spoons and whatnot at her mother-in-law's bidding. The kitchen was soon filled with a pungent aroma.

The telephone in the drawing room began to ring. Savitri went to answer it, hoping it was not Revant crying off. Since Satya had gone back to Canada two weeks before, the only time she stepped out was to attend a bhajan, an evening devoted to singing hymns, being held at the house of one of her mother-in-law's friends.

"Hello!" Mrs. Boothalingam said in her loud, hearty voice. She was a big, bossy woman who had been a friend of the family from time immemorial.

"Hello, auntie," Savitri said, hesitantly. She always felt nervous when she spoke to Mrs. Boothalingam.

"How are you, dear?"

"I'm fine, thank you," Savitri said.

"Have you heard from Satya? How is he?"

"He's fine, thank you."

"Any good news?"

"I beg your pardon." For some reason Savitri was reminded of Bible Study classes at the convent-school she had attended.

"I mean, are you carrying?" Mrs. Boothalingam said.

"No! No!"

"What was Satya doing for two weeks, then? You had better hurry!" Mrs. Boothalingam's turn of phrase often left Savitri speechless. "Don't delay too much. Otherwise you might find it very difficult to conceive later on. Is your mother-in-law at home? I'd like to talk to her, please."

"Hold on, auntie, I'll call her. She is in the kitchen making the tamarind pickle."

"Don't disturb her, in that case. I know how fussy she is about that pickle. I'll call later and extract my pound of relish. Ha! Ha! Ha! Good bye, dear."

"Good bye, auntie," Savitri said with relief. She returned to the kitchen and told her mother-in-law about the call.

"Good," Chandramma said. "Savitri, why don't you go and get ready? Revant will be here any moment. You can help me after you come back."

Savitri had a bath and got into a printed silk sari. She looked both prim and pretty at the same time. Smelling of talcum powder, she sat down on a sofa in the drawing room waiting for Revant.

Soon the doorbell rang, and she jumped up to answer it. Revant was standing at the doorstep, smiling. He had a winning smile and, being aware of it, he flashed it constantly like an ID card.

"Hi! Are you ready?" he said.

"Please come in," she said. "Would you like to have something to drink?" She caught the whiff of nicotine and the manly deo he used.

"No, let's go. I have to meet someone later in the evening."

To Savitri it did indeed seem as if Revant was the kind of young man who had busy evenings: muscular and of medium build, he had light coloured eyes and an appealing seven o'clock shadow, deliberately cultivated. She could well imagine him dropping by at clubs and restaurants every night with a female companion at his elbow.

Chandramma darted out of the kitchen, clucking in her mother-hen fashion. She insisted he should have something to eat and drink.

"We have to leave now. It is getting late, as it is."

Chandramma, not being the kind to take defeat easily, made Revant promise that he would pick up a jar of her pickle after it was made.

"My mother will be thrilled," he said. "She says nobody makes pickles as well as you do, auntie."

Pleased with Revant's blandishments, she returned to the kitchen to give the finishing touch to her pickle.

It was quite late when Savitri returned home. Chandramma, not being very savvy with computers either, did not ask Savitri as to what took her so long. Savitri changed into a nightgown and went into the kitchen to complete her share of the work. A phalanx of empty jars stood on the kitchen counter in battle readiness. Many of these jars would invade various homes and win laurels for Chandramma. Mechanically, Savitri began to pour the pickle into the jars. Her eyes had a faraway look.

* * *

More than two weeks have passed since the day the much-vaunted tamarind pickle was made. Savitri has begun to correspond with Satya, using the neighbourhood Internet kiosk. Satya, in his cheeseparing way, has reduced the long-distance calls he makes to India.

It is the afternoon of a hot and languorous day. Savitri and her mother-in-law are seated in the drawing room watching soap on the TV.

"Would you like to have some lime juice?" Amma asks Savitri, when the programme breaks out into a fit of loud advertising jingles.

Even before Savitri can reply the phone rings. Lowering the TV volume, Savitri picks up the receiver.

"Hello, may I speak to Mrs Savitri Satya Prakash?" asks a strange, high-pitched voice.

"Savitri speaking."

"I'm from Testwell Diagnostics, madam. You report is ready. You may collect it today. Congratulations, madam. The result is positive."

"Thank you," says Savitri, surprised by the sudden burst of joy she feels. "I'll collect the report in the evening."

Savitri puts down the receiver, wondering whether this is what she really wants. She waits for some time not knowing how to break the news to Chandramma. At last, she says: "Amma I have some good news. I'm carrying …"

Chandramma's face lights up with delight. She says: "You must call Satya immediately."

"I'll send him an e-mail," Savitri says.

"We must go to the temple and offer a cocoanut to the gods," Chandramma says. "Please ring up your parents, too. How happy your mother will be!"

The phone rings again. Savitri picks up the receiver. This time round the voice is neither high-pitched nor strange—it's authoritative and only too familiar.

"Hello, Savitri!" Mrs. Boothalingam says. "I want to speak to your mother-in-law at once."

Savitri hands over the phone to her mother-in-law.

"Hello … Durga? I have some good—What! It cannot be true! As usual, I was so careful. I wonder what could have gone wrong. I am so upset. Thank you for letting me know. Bye."

Chandramma puts down the phone, looking perturbed.

"Mrs. Boothalingam says that the tamarind pickle has turned bad," she says. "It's not a good sign at all. Could it be that she used a wet spoon? I really don't understand. It has never happened before."

Chandramma seems to be in a trance. She waddles slowly to the kitchen, murmuring to herself. Lifting the lid of a large crock jar, she peers inside. Savitri's keen eyes follow Amma's actions like those of a director observing an actor during a rehearsal.

"Oh, my god!" she exclaims. "I wonder how it got spoilt. I was so careful, so careful while making the pickle."

Puzzlement furrowing her brow, she turns towards Savitri.

"You were also careful, weren't you?" she asks, pleadingly.

Savitri is silent.

Mango Fool

T

he very thought of the upcoming weekend filled Kavita with dread.

It was Friday evening, and in one more hour her shift would end. She was struggling to arrange the freshly un-packed fall collection in the scant space vacated by a slow-moving summer range. It reminded her of newly arrived immigrants like her family competing to find a niche in an already crowded society. She heard her name called out over the PA system. This was the cue to drop everything and rush to open another cash register to deal with the line-up.

Kavita was 20 years old, slim, small-boned and good-looking. There was that little something about her—per-haps it was the way she dressed or spoke—which suggested that she was new to Canada. After finishing a course in accounting from a local college, she had taken up this job in a new garment store called "Mirabelle" in Mississauga, rather than sit at home and do nothing, while she waited for her parents to decide on whether she could continue her studies.

As Kavita walked up briskly to the checkout, she ran into Joanna, the assistant manager. Joanna was wheeling a buggy filled with returns to the back of the shop.

"All the best for tomorrow," Joanna said without breaking her stride. "Let me know how it goes."

The ceremony being held at Kavita's house was a kind of a prelude to an arranged marriage, where the boy's parents meet the girl's parents. If the boy's family liked the girl's family (to say nothing of the girl), things would lead to an engagement or to the wedding itself. When Kavita spoke to her co-workers about the traditional function, she had neither felt diffident nor sounded self-deprecating. After all, only the other day, Aneesa of Customer Service, sitting in a condo in Etobicoke, had got married over the phone to a groom living in Los Angeles. Nobody in the store had batted so much as an eyelid, at least not publicly.

For an outsider, the very idea of a formal inspection of a bride-to-be might have seemed comical, if not outrageous. Kavita too had shared in her colleagues' amusement at first. But now, as the days wore on, she felt a dull ache in her stomach whenever she thought of the function.

The crowd at the store was larger than usual because of the end of season sale. Kavita stole a quick glance at the large glass front doors. It was the last days of summer; the sun was still out there, but darkness was already tiptoeing in from the east. Anytime now, Father would turn up. He'd position himself outside the glass doors, slightly to one side, from where he could see and be seen. It was only on rare occasions that he volunteered to pick up Kavita; ordinarily, she took a bus home. Tomorrow's function certainly rated as something special, and therefore the extra caution. Of late Father had been saying time and again that nothing must go wrong.

Right from the moment Mrs. Chakravarthy made the tentative proposal for her son Devender, Kavita's parents had been thrown into a tizzy. They had never expected a match, even if it was tentative, to fall into their laps in Canada—looking for a groom was an onerous task even in India. There was a bewildering swirl of activity: consulting elders in India, buying new clothes, going to a beauty spa, and the hectic preparations for the party.

Turning to the next customer, Kavita smiled and uttered the shop-scripted greeting. But the customer merely nodded and, with an I-brook-no-nonsense expression, emptied her shopping basket on to the counter. She was a big, middle-aged South Asian woman, bulging out of her blue jeans and a nondescript top. Most of the garments the woman wanted to buy had red stickers on them. Kavita began to scan the items one by one, quickly, methodically. All the while she was aware of the customer's looming presence—silent but ominous. But when Kavita came to the last piece, a smartly cut beige fall coat, she paused and looked at the label: the codes on the red sticker and the original price-tag did not match.

"Excuse me, ma'am," said Kavita, "this garment doesn't have the right price on it. Actually, it's a new product and it's not on sale."

"What d'ya mean?" the woman said. Her voice was deep and loud, and somehow she seemed to grow in size as she spoke.

"I'm sorry, but I can't sell it to you at the price printed on the sticker."

"If you can't sell it, why do you have it in your shop!"

"There seems to have been a mistake, the sticker belongs to another product—"

"Here, let me have a look," the woman said, grabbing the coat from Kavita. "Are you accusing me of tampering with the tag? How dare you!"

"I didn't say that. Let me call the manager. Perhaps she'll be able to help you." With shaking hands, Kavita reached for the phone on the wall.

"If you think I'm a thief, why don't you call the police?" the woman said, throwing the coat on the counter. She pushed both her wrists towards Kavita, and said: "Come on, put the handcuffs on me."

If the woman's actions were not so obviously threatening, they might even have been funny. But Kavita was in no mood to laugh: her palms felt clammy and the receiver almost slipped out of her hand. The phone kept ringing and ringing. Oh, where in the world was Sharon?

Then Kavita heard the firm voice of her manager, not on the phone but right next to her. Sharon must have witnessed it all on the CCTV console upstairs.

"Let me help you," she said to the customer. Turning to Kavita, whose shift was coming to an end, she said: "Kavita, you can go now if you like."

Kavita turned to look at the front door. It was dark already. In the light of the street lamp, she saw her father staring into the shop. She went to the locker room at the back of the store to collect her handbag and lunch box. On her way out, she saw Sharon stuffing the clothes, including the expensive coat, into a light pink bag with the shop's name written in large pistachio green letters. Sharon must have mollified the customer with a hefty discount; the stern look on the customer's face had yielded to one of smugness.

Sitting in the car, Kavita tried to hold back the tears that were on the verge of spilling out while Father concentrated on negotiating the car through the Friday evening traffic. When the car unsteadily slipped into the highway, he said: "What was that all about?"

Her throat aching with unshed tears, Kavita gave an account of the incident. It was like providing a belated voiceover for a show Father had watched in mute.

"Do you mean she tried to cheat?"

"Most probably," Kavita said, as the dam-gates in her eyes broke and tears rushed down her cheeks. Wiping her eyes with the small lace-edged cotton handkerchief she always carried in her hand bag, she added: "Somebody in the shop could have made the mistake, but the chances are slim."

"Vita, I know she was very rude to you. But you must understand that there are all kinds of people in this world. You've got to learn to get along with them. Don't take the incident to heart. Especially now."

Especially now! When she was going to be married off and would soon start living amidst strangers. Kavita's mouth felt dry, and an unpleasantly familiar heaviness began to settle over her chest. She found it difficult to breathe. No, not now! Especially now, when nothing must go wrong!

Father brought the car to a halt in their driveway. When he switched off the engine, he too heard the clicking. It was as though some anatomical metronome in her lungs were trying to keep time with her laboured breathing. Kavita felt more sorry for Father than for herself.

Father helped her climb the short flight of stairs to the front door. When Mother threw open the door for them, a look of consternation swept over her face even without their having to say a word.

"I knew the wheezing would come on sooner or later—working in a garment shop with all the dust and lint around you! I don't know why you couldn't sit at home until you found a nice office job."

"Padma ..." said Father said to Mother.

They rushed Kavita off to bed. Unable to lie down flat, Kavita leaned back on the two pillows Father had propped up against the headboard. Mother fetched a puffer from the kitchen where she stored medicines, and gave it to Kavita. Trying to take in deep breaths, Kavita hoped her attack would subside soon and she could go to sleep. Tomorrow was a day she didn't want to face; but face it she must, whether she got a wink of sleep or not.

Father returned carrying a glass of water and the medicine their doctor in India had prescribed for her asthma. In the cabinet above the kitchen sink, Mother always kept a stock of prescription drugs, like antibiotics and antihistamines, she had brought from India. Mother had discovered that, not only were medicines expensive in Canada, but the doctors were too fussy when it came to writing prescriptions.

After she took the tablet, Kavita tried to go to sleep. But a few minutes after her parents left the room, her younger brother walked in, carrying a cell phone in his hand and wearing the earphones of an iPod. Jayant was in grade twelve; he got A's in all the subjects, just as she had done. Her parents were hoping that they'd be able to save enough money to send him to university; Kavita had to settle for a community college.

Jayant pulled out an earphone and said: "Are you feeling OK?" He sat down on the bed next to her. It was nice to have him around even though he would rather text than talk to her.

"Are you sending out messages cancelling tomorrow's party, Jay?" Kavita said.

"I wish I could, Vita." Jayant took her hand and squeezed it. "Vita" had been Jayant's rendition of her name when he was a toddler, and the diminutive had stuck. As a child, whenever he was overcome with fraternal love, he would give her a hug and call her his Bournvita. Cadbury's Bournvita was a chocolate-flavoured health drink the two had grown up on. Even now, her mother regularly bought it from an Indian grocery, and gave her son a tall glass to drink up every morning.

Kavita hoped that her father would ring up the Chakravarthys and call off the function but, deep down in her heart, she knew it wouldn't happen. Yet, she could sympathise with her parents. Having been brought up in India, she knew how hard it was to get a daughter married— there were obstacles of social status, dowry, caste, good looks, skin colour, education and God knew what other imponderables.

Her parents and the Chakravarthys did not belong to the same social set. The Chakravarthys owned a chain of dollar shops and lived in a bungalow on Mississauga Road. Rajani Chakravarthy had seen Kavita last October at the Diwali party thrown by an Indian cultural association and spoke to Mother about a possible match for her son.

This made Father who worked as a lead hand in a machine shop so nervous that he took his car and drove past the house where the Chakravarthys lived, just for a look-see. What he saw alarmed him: the house appeared to be seven-gabled, a BMW *and* a Mercedes were sitting on the long and wide driveway. (Who'd have thought there was so much money in dollar shops?) He believed it would be the height of imprudence to give his daughter in marriage to an exceedingly affluent family where she might feel like a misfit or be mistreated.

"They are aware of our social status," Mother said. "Rajani knows that we came to Canada just four years ago. In fact that's our strength. She wants a *bahu* who's not too Canadianized."

"Really?" Father said.

"Rajani's looking for a typical Indian daughter-in-law and also someone who'll not feel too out place in Canada. And I think Kavita fits the requirement to a T."

Before Father could get another bout of cold feet, Mother sent off a photo of Kavita to the Chakravarthys. The picture had been taken on the day they took their oath of Canadian citizenship. Wearing a shimmering green and gold *salwar kameez*, Kavita stood in front of the Canadian flag, a prop that was kept in readiness for the benefit of the newly-anointed citizens. Kavita looked every inch an Indian, and the maple leaf flag in the background, according to Mother, lent her a global appeal.

The next morning when Kavita woke up, she felt tired and groggy. Father and Mother held a war council, sitting at the bottom-edge of her bed. "Should we cancel the function?" Mother asked.

"We shouldn't act in haste," said Father. "This is a chance in a million for Vita."

Kavita, having folded back her legs to make place for her parents, listened to their conversation. She knew her parents were well-meaning, even if a little misguided. She might have protested had she not sensed the deep insecurity they felt, a natural aftershock of immigration.

"This match is a godsend," said Father, who after the initial misgivings had made a complete about turn. Thanks to Mother's perseverance, the proselyte had become more zealous than the prophet. "If it doesn't click, we'll have to start looking for a groom in India. You know how hard that is. And Kavita is so shy and sensitive—she's not the kind of girl who can find a match for herself."

Long after her parents' left the room, Kavita lay in bed unable to sleep. She may not be capable of finding a match for herself, but would she have the guts to say no, if she found the boy unappealing?

Mother returned soon to give Kavita another dose of her tablets from India. And she reappeared at the top of every hour with a basin of cold water to swab Kavita's face.

"You seem to be improving by the minute," Mother said.

This was true; Kavita had certainly begun to feel better. Call it Mother's touch, if you will. Kavita was receiving war despatches continually from downstairs: Jayant had vacuumed the living room or that Father was dusting all the furniture and fixtures. Piece by piece, everything began to fall into place.

But at 3 o'clock in the afternoon, Mother came with her basin of cold water and some bad news. The *shrikand* she had planned to make was a fiasco. *Shrikand* was a special sweet made with sweetened yoghurt and flavoured with a variety of nuts. So Mother had to rush back into the kitchen to rustle up some *sheera*, a simple sweet made from semolina and sugar—the only dessert she could make at short notice.

"Not a problem," Mother had said and patted Kavita's cheek, dismissing the possibility that the mishap could be interpreted as a bad omen. "I heard that Rajani's not good at making Indian sweets. They always have to make do with shop-made sweets. I'm sure everything will work out ok in the end."

However the mango *fool*, a drink made with braised green mangoes, turned out to be excellent. Not for a moment had Kavita doubted that outcome, even though the recipe was laborious. Mango *fool* was Father's favourite drink.

In vain did Kavita try not to think about the evening ahead, or the fate that awaited her if everything went well. On one of her frequent sorties into Kavita's bedroom, Mother had said: "Your father and I had never set our eyes on each other until the day of our wedding. But wouldn't you call us a happily married couple?"

Kavita wanted Devender to find her so unattractive that he'd muster enough spunk to say no to the match. She was leery of rushing headlong into matrimony, and this would buy her time. But she hurriedly recanted her wish—if Devender were to reject her, her parents would feel disappointed, even humiliated. On the other hand, what if she didn't take a liking to Devender? Would her parents listen to her rather than remain blindsided by the Chakravarthys' ritzy lifestyle? Either way she would be condemned to participate in such functions again and again until her marriage was settled.

It's my life and I shouldn't let others manipulate me, Kavita told herself. *If I don't like the match for any reason, I should speak up.*

But how would her parents react? Confrontation was something she was congenitally wired to shy away from. She wasn't sure about Mother, but she knew in her heart that Father would, despite everything, stand by her.

Later in the evening, the family assembled in the drawing room. Kavita looked beautiful, even if a little tired, in a red *ghagra* and *choli* embroidered with gold thread. She wore an imitation ruby necklace, and ear- and finger-rings to match. She felt nervous and forgot all about her resolve to think independently for herself. Uppermost in her thoughts was the need to make a good impression and thereby not let her parents down.

The tallboy clock her father had bought at Wal-Mart tolled six times. A few seconds later the door bell rang. The moment the Chakravarthys stepped into the house, excited greetings were bandied about like battle cries.

The Chakravarthys looked like characters from an Indian soap: tall, good looking and ostensibly rich. Rajani's smile outshone the diamonds that adorned various parts of her body: throat, nose, ears and fingers. She was dressed in an electric blue and gold Benares silk sari, and looked vaguely familiar. Mr. Chakravarthy wore a business suit, as though he had come to attend a board meeting. Devender was thin and tall, even taller than his father and, though he was smiling, there was something cowed about his expression.

Kavita's eyes went to the pink gift bag Rajani was holding in her hand. It had "Mirabelle" written in a pale shade of green, the colour of Mother's mango *fool*. Recognition dawned on Kavita. She remembered where she had seen

Rajani before. She was the same obnoxious customer who had been rude to her. She felt her skin break into goose bumps as a wave of fear and revulsion swept over her.

By the time she accepted the gift from a sparkling, smiling Rajani, Kavita had partly recovered from the shock. She stepped forward and—in a voice so loud that it surprised her, and made Father direct a questioning gaze—she said: "Mrs. Chakravarthy, I think we've met before ..."

In the Dark

The young woman was licked, fair and square. She began to chew the end of her ballpoint pen. He could see from the corner of his eye that she had already got the fourth letter. The black and white grid was nearly full, her neat lettering filling most of the blank squares.

She had got in at the Old Mill station in Toronto where the subway train came up out into the open, as if for a breather, before diving back into the earth again. The girl had given a quick glance around the car, their eyes meeting briefly. She had headed to the vacant seat next to him, brushing past his knees.

Pulling out a folded newspaper from her bag, she had at once started tackling the half-done crossword puzzle. She was Asian and her skin was the shade of old ivory. He could smell the perfume she wore.

When the train stopped at High Park, he looked at his watch. The time was a quarter to four and the afternoon rush had not yet begun. The date was the 14th of August. The following day was his wedding anniversary, and he did not even have a clue as to what he would give his wife. Last year he had bought Shalini a bunch of flesh-pink roses and a small flask of Chanel No. 5.

The girl next to him was still wrestling with the puzzle. Imperceptibly, he edged closer to the girl. He felt the side of his thigh lightly touching her. He squinted at the newspaper:

16. Courtship of the lower extremities, walks that is (7)

When the train stopped at Bathurst, three teenagers got in. They were all dressed in black from head to toe, and wore silver jewellery. The only girl in the group even had her nails and mouth painted black. Dev couldn't fathom what fashion statement they were making, but in India they might have been mistaken for pilgrims for Sabarimalai—a temple in south India. These devotees kept off sex and alcohol—much like Dev. He had stopped buying liquor because he was hard pressed for money and, as to sex, it was a non-event. The train reached Spadina but the answer continued to elude the girl. He could feel her knee pressing against his thigh. Or was he imagining things? He leaned sideways and whispered into her ear: "Footsie."

"What?!"

"The answer to the clue, young lady."

The girl turned to look at him. A flicker of an elfin smile lit up his good-looking face. Wordlessly she returned to her crossword and began to fill the remaining squares, deliberating on every letter, as though she was not prepared to accept his "word" as gospel.

"That's awesome of you!" she said, at last.

"It's nothing."

"This is the first time that I've managed to fill in all the words."

"Congratulations!"

"All thanks to you," she said, as she stuffed the newspaper into her handbag. "Do you also enjoy doing crossword puzzles?"

"Yes," Dev said. "But I don't get the chance to do them, nowadays."

"Too busy to find time?"

"On the contrary, I've plenty of time on my hands," he said. "The daily newspaper is a luxury we can't afford. I'm out of job right now. What do you do, if I may ask?"

"I'm studying to be a fashion designer."

"Wow!"

"I'm Anne," she said.

"I'm Dave," said Dev said, hardening the first letter of his name.

"Are you from Pakistan?"

"No. India."

"Sorry! It's hard to make out the difference."

"I'm not surprised," Dev said. "Are you from China?"

"No," she said. "Laos."

"There we go again!"

The train stopped at Bay, and a lady with a little girl in a stroller got off. Dev was reminded of his children who were in the care of a neighbour. Shalini had instructed him to return home as soon as possible to save on the babysitting fee.

The doors closed to the tinkling bells and the train slid out of the station. The lights in the car blinked twice and the train slowed down for no ostensible reason. Though it picked up a little speed, it pulled in hesitantly into Yonge station rather than breezing in as it usually did.

Surprisingly, there was very little light in the station. Nobody rushed to the door to board the train though there were people milling about on the platform, looking like ghosts in the eerie light. A few of the passengers got off the train, but others continued to sit, looking out of the windows with a perplexed air.

An announcer came on the line: "There's a problem with—"

Dev did not wait to hear him to complete the sentence.

"There's something seriously wrong," he said, rising from his seat. "Come, let's get off the train!"

"Shouldn't we wait to find out what's—"

"It's best if we leave now," Dev said. "Hurry!"

Anne followed Dev as he bounded out of the train. Soft light filtered down on to the platform from god knows where. It was more as if they were underwater rather than underground.

"What do think may have happened?" asked Anne.

"Honestly, I don't know. My gut tells me something is amiss—call it my survival instinct."

"I hope you're right."

"You know what," Dev said. "My hope is that I'm wrong."

They raced up a stalled escalator and squirmed past the turnstile. A small group of people had gathered in front of the ticket counter.

"Should we find out more?" Anne said.

"Let's get the hell out of here first," Dev said, walking on towards the exit. They took the stairs that led to Yonge Street, ascending like a pair of divers reaching for the surface. Outside, the scene was amazing. The sidewalks were choc a bloc with people and cars were lined up on the road, bumper to bumper. Pedestrians were crossing the roads anywhere and everywhere, sidling between motion-less cars.

Anne looked up at the sky, as if half-expecting to see signs of doom. But it was picture perfect—a serene expanse of blue framed by the tops of tall buildings.

"Hey buddy," Dev asked a passerby, "what's happening?"

"The world's coming to an end, that's what, bro!" the man said, without breaking stride.

"The traffic lights are not working," Dev said to Anne. "And all the shops look so dark inside."

"I don't see a single cab, anywhere!" Anne said.

"My house is nearby," Dev said. "Why don't you come home with me? Later, you can take a taxi."

"I'd rather not. I want to get home as soon as I can."

"Where do you live?"

"Scarborough," Anne said with listlessness in her tone.

"Scarborough! That would be one long walk."

Anne was silent, as though she was grappling with yet another of her crossword clues. "I'll have to leave you now," Dev said. "Take care!"

"Wait," Anne said hesitantly. "I hope your place isn't too far away."

"No, not too far. Let's keep talking as we walk, that way you'll not notice the distance."

"What shall we talk about?"

"For a start," Dev said, "do you miss Laos?"

"I've never been there."

"Were you born in Canada, then?"

"No, in Thailand. My father and mother had to flee Laos."

"During the Pol Pot regime?"

"No. That's Cambodia."

"Oops. Sorry!"

"Never mind. My father had been a government official in Laos and, because he was a Royalist, the Pathet Lao were hunting for him. My parents swam across the Mekong one night and eventually made it to Thailand."

"Wow! That's some story. I hope things got better for your parents after coming to Canada."

"In some ways, yes and in other ways, no. My father never managed to get a decent job. Not knowing the language and all that. My mother still works as a cleaning lady. My father passed away a few years ago. How have things worked out for you in Canada?"

* * *

Before moving to Canada, Dev and Shalini were living in Dubai, an oil-rich emirate hungry for workers from poorer countries of Asia. The three years Dev spent there were the most productive ones of his life. He had earned enough money to build himself a palatial house in his home-town—in India, having a house of your own rated as one of the highest achievements of your life. And Shalini, the quintessential housewife, did her bit by presenting Dev with two strapping sons, twins at that.

Small wonder, then, that Dev felt like a traveller who had reached his destination much too soon. In his restless-ness, he did what many successful South Asians in the

Middle East were doing: he applied for immigration to Canada.

Two years later, on a grey, wet afternoon, Dev along with his wife and two children landed in Toronto's Pearson airport. They rented an apartment in a downtown high-rise and furnished it to the hilt. They bought a snazzy little Mazda and had a whale of a time visiting places like Niagara Falls, Thousand Islands, Wasaga Beach and whatnot.

They bought their groceries, at Shalini's insistence, from places with names like Fortino's and Michael-Angelo's—no run of the mill grocery shops ever for them. Shalini never tired of telling her new-found friends, how even if the prices were *a little* high, the stuff was *really* good. They liked all those baked products: croissants, doughnuts and muffins. Dev in particular had taken a fancy to fruit-filled pies: they were always flaky and fresh, and when his tongue rolled over the gooey filling, it tasted like heaven. They reminded him of the confectionery in the five-star hotels he had worked in.

Once they were comfortably settled in Toronto, Dev started to look for a job. Only then did he touch base with reality. He had been working as a Banquet Manager in a hotel in Dubai but here, try as he might, he couldn't find a job in a hotel. Not even a bell boy's. Being new to Canada he hadn't yet built a network of friends and compatriots who might have helped him. In desperation, Dev started working at a gas station for eight dollars an hour. But he soon called it quits, when the owner wanted him to pay for the gas self-serve customers stole. Shalini toyed with the idea of taking up a job, but having two children in preschool meant she'd have to shell out a small fortune for daycare, and this

defeated the very purpose of going to work. Soon their
funds in Canada began to evaporate like a puddle of rain-
water under the Arabian sun.

When the twins started attending school full time,
Shalini looked for a job. With a referral from one of her
friends she netted a job in a warehouse where she had to
pack toys. She was paid a princely sum of nine dollars and
fifty cents an hour and even received medical benefits
(though with a big annual deductible and a low coinsur-
ance). But it was better than nothing, especially since Dev
couldn't stick to a job for long. They traded their penthouse
apartment for a dingy basement, and their sporty car gave
way to an elderly Toyota which Shalini, being the primary
breadwinner, drove to work. Inevitably, they began to buy
their groceries from places like *Food Basics* and *No Frills*.

Things began to change in other ways too. One morning, as Shalini was preparing to leave for the grocery shop,
Dev asked her bring him a strawberry pie. Shalini returned
from the mall with a perforated plastic box containing fresh
strawberries and dumped it on the table in front of him.

"You should stop eating those disgusting pies," she said.
"You're putting on too much weight. Eat some fresh fruit
instead."

Dev could only gape at her in reply—his assessment of
his place in the universe changed forever.

* * *

"My house is only two blocks down the road," Dev said.

"Am I glad to hear it!" Anne said.

"Do you mind if I pick up something from a shop?"

They went into a convenience store. The place was jam-packed with people buying things like bread, butter, bottled water and flashlight batteries. Dev picked up a strawberry pie.

As they stood in the long line, they heard people talking about the black out.

"I believe that the entire province is without electricity."

"No. All of North America, in fact."

"I'm sure it is the work of terrorists!"

Once outside, they started to walk again. At last, they came to the street where Dev lived. Tucked between two houses was a flagstone path which led to his basement apartment.

Dev unlocked the door and stepped inside.

"Isn't your wife home?" Anne asked.

"No," Dev said. Then added with a chuckle: "I've sent her packing!"

"What do you mean?"

"Well she works as a packer, that's all. Come in. There's nobody at home. Does it scare you?"

"No. I've never heard of a serial killer who had a passion for strawberry pies or—"

"Or what?"

"Or solves crossword clues in a jiffy."

"Good to know."

"Where are your children?"

"They're with a Pakistani baby-sitter who lives nearby. She keeps kids after school until their parents can pick them up. During vacation, we leave the kids for the entire day. Fortunately, she doesn't charge much."

It was almost pitch dark inside. Anne started climbing

down the steep staircase. The door behind her closed of its own accord. She cried out: "I can't see anything!"

"Here, grab my hand," Dev said. "Ouch! That's not my hand!"

Holding on to each other they tottered down the steps. When they reached the bottom, Dev bent his head and tried to kiss Anne.

"No," she said turning her head away. Anne felt something hard at her navel. It was the carry-bag containing the strawberry pie.

"Stay right here and don't move," Dev said. "I'll go and look for a candle."

Dev moved away from her and melted into the shadows. At the far end of the room, sunlight dribbled wanly into the house from a small window high up in the wall. Anne heard the faint sigh of a match, and then golden light bloomed from the kitchen. Dev returned with a candle stuck over an inverted coffee-mug in one hand and a knife in the other.

In the flickering light his face looked attractive, like that of a brooding romantic hero in an old black and white movie. He placed the mug and the knife on the dining table. In the half-light, the furniture around them looked like crouching beasts. As Anne walked up to the table, her shadow on the wall followed her with gawky, exaggerated movements.

Dev went back into the kitchen and returned with a bottle of wine and two plastic glasses. He poured some wine and offered it to Anne.

"I'm not sure I want one," she said.

"Come on. Let's celebrate! Don't make a fuss. Today's a very special day."

"What makes you say that?" Anne said, taking the glass

gingerly and seating herself at the dining table. "Is it because of the blackout?"

"No, for the first time you've completed a crossword puzzle."

"Not true. You finished it for me."

"You protest too much, lady. Let me think up of another reason. OK, today is *not* my wedding anniversary!"

Anne took a sip of the wine. It had the full-bodied aroma of acrylic. She said: "How long have you been married?"

"Seven years. "Seven l-o-n-g years."

"That explains many things," Anne said.

"What about yourself? You're not single, are you? You don't look the type."

"Well, at the moment I am."

"What do you mean by 'at the moment'?"

"I was serious about someone," she said. "But it fizzled out."

"That's too bad. What happened?"

"My boyfriend would call me his Annelida," she said. "He was majoring in life sciences. At first, I thought that it was a term of endearment. Need I say anything more?"

"That worm!" Dev said and laughed. "What a fool he is to break up with a beautiful, intelligent and courageous young lady."

"Courageous? Not that I claim to be beautiful and intelligent either."

"Well, it needs some pluck to accompany a stranger to his house, and have a glass of wine."

"I'm far from a fearless person. Frankly, the ambience," she said, pointing at the surrounding darkness, "I find it very spooky."

"Nevertheless, you are still here, taking small sips of

the wine. But what do you think of me? Give me three words which describe me. Be honest."

Anne tilted her head to one side, and said: "You are quite attractive, definitely sharp, and ... er ... not very dangerous."

"Really? For some reason the last attribute doesn't flatter me. Men don't like to be considered safe."

He picked up the knife and, making a show of testing its sharpness, began to cut slices out of the pie. He extended the box towards Anne. She selected a piece and took a tentative bite.

"Shalini detests it," Dev said.

Munching the slice of the oversweet pie, Anne could sympathise with his wife.

He raised the bottle and said: "Would you like to have some more?"

"I'm fine," Anne said, looking at her watch.

Dev began to speak wistfully about his life in the Middle East. How he had received ten times of what he had been earning in India, and tax-free to boot. Of the parties they would be invited to every weekend, of the reckless shopping sprees and of the long road trips in the desert.

"You're bored," Dev said.

"Not really," she said, trying to conceal a yawn with the slice of strawberry pie she had in her hand.

"So that was a brief history of my life in Dubai. Now I have to come to terms with my situation in Canada."

"Can't you go back?"

"You can never really go back," he said, bitterness leaching into his voice. "Things have changed, people have changed, and Dubai too, I bet."

The airless room had become hot and stuffy. Anne

started to feel the beginnings of a headache. She had spent more time than she had planned to, and wished she was on her way home. The candle was reduced to a stump, and the melted wax looked like frozen tears on the side of the coffee-mug.

Then they heard a scrabbling sound coming from the head of the staircase—as though someone was trying to open the door. Both of them turned to look. The door opened slowly. A shadowy form started climbing down the stairs, but stopped midway. Hard on its heels another shadow appeared, forcing the former to resume its descent.

"You have come back early," a female voice said.

"You too," Dev said, as if he were returning a greeting.

Anne half-expected Dev to say: "Quick, hide!"

Entering the ring of light, the two figures loomed over the seated pair.

"We seem to have company," the woman said, furtively buttoning her blouse with one hand.

"This is my wife, Shalini," Dev said. "This is Anne."

"Hi," Anne said nervously.

"How are you, Raj?" Dev said. "I've not seen you for ages."

The man wiped his mouth with the back of his hand. He said: "I-I've been busy."

"I can see that," Dev said.

The man giggled. Shalini opened her mouth to speak. But no words came out. The red lipstick she wore was smudged around her mouth. She looked as if she had gorged herself on a strawberry pie, behind her husband's back.

That Which is Written

No Signal. Two small shit-coloured words at the bottom of a screen bathed in violet light. Less than five minutes to go, and here I am struggling to make my laptop in sync with the projector. I feel annoyed and a tad foolish. My firm has invited sales agents from across Toronto to inform them of our new compensation structure. Most of the 50 odd seats are occupied. The aroma of coffee and muffins hangs in the air.

My mobile rings. In the board room, its tinny ringtone sounds loud as a steam-whistle. I look at the number. Not again! I excuse myself and take the call outside the room.

"Rahul's class teacher Mrs. Downey would like to meet you after school today," the assistant from my son's school says. "Will you be able to make it?"

"I'll come over." What mischief has Rahul gotten into this time? In a way I'm relieved: on two previous occasions I had to leave my work and rush to the school because of medical emergencies.

When I return to the meeting, the screen is full of Microsoft icons swimming in a sea of green. The problem with the projector has been sorted out. Probably by Terri-Ann, my manager, but it makes me look incompetent somehow. I start the presentation. Unbidden, thoughts churn in my head: *What had Rahul done? Had he gotten into a fight? Was it something to do with his homework? Could it be his nose-diving grades?*

In the afternoon, I leave early. "Family comes first, Sid. Work can wait," Terri-Ann had reassured me earlier in the day. She too is a single parent, but she doesn't appear as besieged with problems as I do. It's easier for a woman, I tell myself.

On the way to my son's school a blue Beamer cuts me off. Sounding the horn, I try to give chase. I miss my intersection and so I have to go around the block. I'm ten minutes late. But finding Rahul's classroom is no hassle; I'm a frequent visitor there.

Mrs. Downey and Rahul are seated at a low round table. Mrs. Downey's going through a pile of books. She wears glasses with thick, dark frames. Tall and heavily built, she makes the Grade 3 furniture around her look like things from a doll's house. She's only a supply teacher, standing in for the home room teacher who went on mat leave. Mrs. Downey took over in the middle of the term, and coping with a rambunctious bunch of nine-year-old devils is no picnic.

Rahul's doing a jigsaw with an unconcerned air. He has his mother's face, gentle, serene, and with almond shaped eyes. But his strong lower jaw with a cleft is definitely from me. When he sees me, he drops the piece he is holding and leans back—erect, alert.

Mrs. Downey rises and comes around the table to

shake hands with me. As I negotiate my butt onto a tiny chair, she says: "Mr. Kumar, I don't enjoy calling parents over to listen to my complaints about their children. I know how busy you are, but Rahul—he has misbehaved *again*."

I wince at the emphasis on the last word. Mrs. Downey has had it in for Rahul from the time he corrected her when she had misidentified an African elephant as Indian. She has never forgiven him.

"Look at what he's done," she says and hands me something I take for a toy.

But the thingamajig is a small 4″ × 4″ erasable white board with handle. One of those cheap things children bring to school, and then don't bother to take it back home. A coiled plastic wire attaches a dry-erase marker to the board. In the centre of the writing area are four words in red: "fuck You , Kevin Williams." The first 'u' looks more like an 'a', but there is no mistaking—it's Rahul's handwriting. They glow as if they're written with LEDs.

"I notice a spelling mistake," I say. "And the use of upper and lower cases is incorrect."

"Mr. Kumar!" Mrs. Downey says.

"OK, OK, I see what you mean. But there could be an innocent explanation."

Rahul steals a quick glance at me—after all I rarely bat for him. But then I didn't like to agree with Mrs. Downey right away.

"Using the F-word in school is a very serious matter. And *writing* it ... it's, it's inexcusable."

"Rahul, did you do this?" I ask. My son opens his mouth, but no words come out. I raise my voice: "Did you do this?"

"It was ... it was Daniel who did it. I ... I only—"

"Did you hear that?" Mrs. Downey says, butting into our man-to-man conversation. Like a pugilist jumping into the ring, fists flailing. "He's always blaming others, even when the offensive line is undeniably in his handwriting. He never takes responsibility for his actions." I sigh, Mrs. Downey's last comment has such a familiar ring to it. I've heard it so often in my life that it has as good as become my family's motto. Turning towards my son, I say: "Rahul, apologise to your teacher for what you've done."

Rahul opens his mouth. Like a fish in an aquarium. Neither words nor bubbles come out.

"Rahul, you're going to be in real trouble, if you don't apologise to Mrs. Downey."

"I've said, I'm sorry."

"Mr. Kumar, this isn't about apologising. I've been observing Rahul, his behaviour is going from bad to worse—"

"Mrs. Downey, you've told me that before. Given the circumstances, I'm doing all I can."

"Mr. Kumar, I think Rahul needs some expert help."

"Do you mean counselling?" I ask. I've no faith in such things. Hogwash, if you ask me. But I say: "I'll look into it." Jotting down the 1-800 number Mrs. Downey gives me, I leave with Rahul.

There was a time when I didn't know how to make a cup of coffee. But now, I've learnt to cook, even downloading Indian recipes from the internet. I drop off and pick up Rahul from school every day, I see to his homework, do the laundry, vacuum the house.

When I stop at an intersection, I burst out: "Next time you get into this kind of trouble at school, I'll beat the shit out of—" I look over my shoulder at Rahul. He has fallen asleep, his mouth slightly open. Rahul always sits in the back, leaving the front passenger seat unoccupied, as if for his mother to return to. His mother is never going to return.

* * *

A little over a year ago, on a bleak winter afternoon, Reena was involved in a single car collision. That very morning we had had one of our nasty rows. Reena wanted to go to India to attend her cousin's wedding. We were strapped for cash. I hadn't received my quarterly bonus because of poor sales. Reena's job was an hourly one—if she didn't go to work, she didn't get paid.

"Right now, Reena, you can't afford a holiday."

"Sid, we have to maintain good relationships with our extended family. It won't look good if I don't go to the wedding. It's the first marriage in my aunt's family. Besides it's off season, an air ticket won't be very expensive."

"We have to pay for two tickets, mind you. You know you will have to take Rahul with you. I can't take care of him on my own."

"It's time you learned to take care of Rahul. Men in Canada help out with taking care of children."

"Maybe some time in the future. I can't learn that skill overnight. Moreover the bank jacked up the mortgage rate last month. Seriously, I just can't pony up cash for a jaunt to India right now."

Reena was upset but there was little either of us could do. It was Reena's habit to get into her car and drive along unfrequented roads to improve her mood.

I got the call from a hospital in the outskirts of Toronto

about Reena's life threatening injuries when I was in the middle of a meeting. I was already on my way when I remembered about Rahul. I made a U-turn and drove to his school to pick him up. The drive to the hospital seemed so long, as if we were journeying to land's end. Wreathed in mist, the hospital was dark and unwelcoming. We parked the car in the desolate lot and walked up to the building. The snow shone like broken glass under the street lamps which were few and far between. But inside, the atmosphere was kept bright and warm as a hothouse, as though to better preserve the sick and the incapacitated. But Reena was already dead when we arrived.

I still do not know how in my shell-shocked condition I managed to make arrangements for the body to be moved to Toronto, like as if I was freight-forwarding an unwieldy piece of furniture. On our way home, I broke the news of his mother's death to Rahul who was puzzled by the seemingly pointless journey.

"What's the meaning of passed away?"

"She has gone to sleep, and will not wake up for a long, long time."

"Do you mean she died?" Rahul asked, kayoing me with his choice of words. "Won't I see her again?"

He started to cry, while I carried unshed tears in my heart, where they had turned into a heavy piece of ice.

We performed Reena's last rites at a Hindu funeral home in a Toronto suburb. Except for the hymns which sounded like Bollywood tunes, it might have been a Christian service. Weighed down by grief and guilt, I did like an automaton what the priest bid me to do. The thing I remember most is the sight of masses and masses of blood-red roses in the casket smothering Reena. Reena had loved flowers, but I had not been buying them as often as I used to—I was too busy with my work to remember all the occasions.

Reena's parents came from India for the funeral. They stayed with us for two weeks, confining themselves indoors as though the RCMP had put them under house arrest. When the day of their departure was near, my father-in-law said to me: "Would you like to send Rahul to India with us? Just for a few months, you know. It will give you time to settle in."

I had been wondering about Rahul's future. After his mother's death he had become very quiet. It was good in a way. I had expected him to snivel and ask: "Where is Mummy?" or "I want Mummy!"

As a new and unwilling single parent I felt let down, and even angry with life. I didn't relish the thought of handing over Rahul to my in-laws. However daunting it was, I had to take care of Rahul myself. No amount of piety and tears would bring Reena back—the moving finger wrote and moved on.

"It's not easy for a man," my mother-in-law chipped in, "to bring up a child all by himself."

Rahul ran over and squeezed himself into the space on the sofa next to me. "I don't want to go to India," he said. "I want to stay with Daddy."

* * *

Every time Mrs. Downey points out Rahul's shortcomings to me, I feel chastened, as though she is pointing at flaws in me. I'm under pressure to do something about it.

"How could you use the F word in class?" I tell Rahul. "Don't you know such things are unacceptable? You will not get any TV time for one week."

Though there's no change in Rahul's expression, I can sense he's relieved. Even overjoyed, perhaps—he must have been expecting to be leathered.

"No TV time for one month is what you deserve," I say. "I'm letting you off this time easily this time. You've behaved very badly, Rahul."

Rahul says something that sounds like "Uh". It occurs to me then how little Rahul and I have been having by way of conversation. *Rahul, put on your socks, it's getting late!* "Uh." *Hurry up, finish your dinner!* "Uh-uh." *Turn down the TV, can't you see I'm working?* "Uh."

I call the number Mrs. Downey gave me. A recorded message, spoken like an airline attendant, asks me to leave a message. But when the social worker from child and family services calls back, we are not at home. I try again, with ditto result. Anyway, it's my considered opinion that counselling is just plain bullshit, a waste of good money, even if my health insurance covers the cost.

This is not the first time that I have been advised to seek counselling ...

* * *

When Reena and I got married, we were the toast of our in-laws' family. They made much of us and invited us to every party and festival. They were of great help too when we set up our home in New Delhi, where I was posted then. But for them, we couldn't have afforded appliances like a washing machine or a dish washer. The first year of our marriage was unalloyed bliss.

But once Reena's younger sister Asha got married, suddenly there were more claimants to my in-laws' attention. Asha gave birth to two children in as many years and our parents-in-law's interest in us began to wane. Reena and I had only a series of miscarriages to show by way of our marital performance.

Ugly quarrels were flaring up between Reena and me, set off by the most inconsequential of remarks. Like the time Reena said: "Shall we go to see *Devdas*?"

"Is it a good film?"

"Asha and Sanjay liked it."

"Are those two great judges of cinema?"

"I never said that. If you don't want go by what they say, it's up to you. But you don't have to speak about them in that tone."

"I'll damn well speak in whatever tone I wish about anybody."

That's how it was, and the strain told on my working life and I found myself not making any headway in my career either. I was passed over for promotion on two occasions.

One day my father-in-law took me aside; he always behaved as if he had proprietorial rights over me.

"Siddhu, for a long time, I've been wanting to talk to you," he said. "Have you and Reena ever considered going in for counselling?"

"I think counselling is a lot of bull," I said.

"If you ask me—"

"I'm not asking you," I said. My father-in-law looked as if I had punched his face, and he never raised the matter again.

The way people talked and behaved one would think I was responsible for every wrong in the world. They were always ready with advice and, if for some reason they couldn't come up with it, they suggested counselling. Anyone would think they were spotters for shrinks.

I was fed up with life in India. All around me, friends and relatives were leaving for places like the US, Australia and New Zealand. I got in touch with an immigration firm. They helped me apply for immigration to Canada.

"Do you think things will improve if we go to Canada?" Reena asked.

"I think a change of scene would do us good," I said. "But it will not be that soon. The consultant said it may take a couple of years to get the Canadian visa and landing papers."

Reena seemed only half-convinced about immigration doing any good to our relationship. I was the sole bread winner to all intents and purposes. Reena was working in a florist's shop just to while away the time and because she liked the idea of working with flowers all around her—but her salary was a pittance. So she didn't have much say, besides she must have believed that putting as much physical distance as possible between me and her family would reduce the discord between the two of us.

A year later, after many frustrating rounds of treatment at a fertility clinic, Rahul was born. The birth of a son brings a certain cachet to the parents in society, and we recovered some of our social standing. After all Asha and Sanjeev had only daughters. I took it as a good omen. Soon afterwards we received the landing papers from the Canadian High Commission.

* * *

We are already into December, a month of snows, squalls and staff parties. It's more than a month since I met Mrs. Downey, and I've not been able to make contact with the counsellor, though we played telephone tag for a few days.

December is also the time for the annual performance appraisal at work. Terri-Ann feels that I am not giving one hundred percent to my job. I sit in front of her going through the appraisal sheet. Terri-Ann has the spacious corner room. Her office table is large and custom-made with expensive-looking knick-knacks deployed on it. Leaning back on her overstuffed executive leather chair, she says: "You need to be more focussed on results, Sid."

In a fit of pique, I send out my resume to hiring agencies which specialise in the financial services industry. A few interviews are set up. Though business is slow thanks to the mortgage crisis in the USA, there are openings in remote places like Okanagan and Regina. The way I'm feeling right now, I'm prepared to move to Yellowknife or Whitehorse.

One busy afternoon, just before the yearly closing date, my phone rings. Absently I pick up the receiver instead of allowing it to ring itself into the voicemail.

"Hi, I'm Rosalita. I'm glad I could get you. We've been leaving messages for each other."

"I'm sorry," I say. "What's this about?"

"You wanted counselling for your son."

"Oh! Yes, of course."

"Would you like to make an appointment?"

"Let me look at my calendar. I'm sorry. I'm very busy all this week. Can I call you sometime next week and let you know when we can meet?"

"Whenever you wish," she says, sounding disappointed. "We're always here to help you."

In the week before Christmas, I receive a call from the head of the hiring agency.

"Sid? It's Bob. Congratulations! They've selected you for their Calgary office."

"Calgary?"

"I know it's a far cry from Toronto, but a change of scene would be good for you."

"I think so too, Bob."

"They'd like you to come on board a-s-a-p."

"I'll think it over and let you know tomorrow when I can start."

In the evening, Rahul brings home two envelopes. It's the last day before the school closes for the holiday season. One of the envelopes contains a report card. For the first time since Reena's death, Rahul gets an A in one of the subjects, though it's only in Visual Arts. I tell myself, I must give him a hug—but Rahul has already escaped to his room. The last time he brought home the report card, I had said: "Rahul, I only see a swarm of B's!"

The second envelope contains a class photo. Twenty-five beaming children, the tall ones standing, short ones crouching. Mrs. Downey stands on one side like a monolith, her face creased with a superior smile. The children's names are provided at the bottom, left to right, row by row: *James Fast, Zainab Hussain, Anne Wong, Manuelo Sanchez, Sanat Wickramasinghe, Ankur Patel, Weixing Zang, Olivia Grant, Kevin Williams, Ashfack Youssef.*

I stop short. Two of the names, because of their juxta-position, ring a bell. I read the names again. Kevin Williams and Ashfack Youssef. I recall the incident of the white board and the two offensive words on it. I remember that the 'u' in the first word looked more like an 'a'.

"Rahul!" I call out. "Where are you?"

Rahul sidles into the living room. He has that what-have-I-done-now look on his face.

"Can you tell me how you came to have those two words and Kevin's name on the white board? I think it has something to do with the name Ashfack Youssef."

Rahul took some time to answer. "Daniel and I decided to write the names of ... of all the noobs in the class."

"What's a noob?"

"A noob is a ... a—"

"Never mind, go on."

"I wrote Ashfack's and Kevin's names. Then Daniel, he ... he ..."

"What did he do?"

"He wiped out most of Ashfack's name, and changed the 'a' into a 'u'. Daniel thought it was a big joke."

In spite of myself, I laugh. It is so egregiously silly, yet—

"But Mrs. Downey didn't think it was funny," Rahul says.

"You ought to have explained it to her."

"I wanted to ... but she didn't give me the chance."

Neither did I, for that matter. "Come here," I say. I put my hand around his shoulders, and draw him to close. "I'm sorry, Rahul."

That night I sleep fitfully. At 2 o'clock I wake up and can't go back to sleep I put on the TV—it comes alive with an explosion of sound and light. I think of my neighbour—I live in a semi with walls made of cardboard. What the fuck, let him pound on the wall first, I'll lower the volume then. But having second thoughts I put the TV on closed caption mode. I watch the movie—about a guy who can predict what's going to happen in the next five minutes and then take corrective action—without paying much attention, though I wonder if my life would have turned out differently if I had that unique ability. In the wee hours of the morning the show seems remote and unreal, and my mind is mostly on Rahul. I have to admit, he too is having a rough a time in life. To understand him better, I must try to put myself in his shoes. Empathising with others isn't something that comes easily to me. On reflection, my life seems to be all about promotions, increments, bonuses ... and self pity. When I look back, there isn't a single person with whom I was on cordial terms for long. Whether it is in Canada or India, I have always had issues, in my professional as well as my personal life, and yet not even once did I try to seek help, or try to change. Bull-headed, my relatives, friends and teachers used to say to my face when I was young.

I shake my head—this was meant to be about Rahul, but as usual I got deflected into thinking about my own situation. I suppose it is not easy to change your view of life all of a sudden. I realise I've been very disloyal. I had not stood by Rahul, and made no attempt to find out what had really happened. Convicting someone without a fair trial, that's what I did. Rahul needs a more sympathetic and caring father. Could I ever be such a parent?

The next morning, I drop off Rahul at his baby sitter's place and go to work. Forgetting all about Bob and the job in Calgary, I call Rosalita. We speak for 15 minutes about the services they offer before I set up an appointment. But it's not for Rahul, it's for me.

For A Place in the Sun

very weekday morning on his way to work, Ananth took the elevator to the basement level of his apartment block and walked up the underground passage that led directly to the "The Path".

The Path is a subterranean system of passages that runs for miles in downtown Toronto. More muddling than a maze, it's lined with over a thousand shops which sell food, wine, clothes, jewellery, books, music, and flowers—in fact, except for the sun, everything under it.

Ananth had a pleasant—some might even say good-looking—face. His sideburns were touched with grey, making him look older than his 30-odd years. He worked as a sales associate at a small electronics shop along The Path.

Ananth walked briskly, glancing at the shop displays now and then, the joys of window-shopping as yet un-diminished even though he had been doing the same thing for nearly two years. He loved to be on The Path at this time of the day when it was deserted and a church-like hush hung over the place. The shops were only now being opened one by one, and the wall-eyed look that haunted The Path during the nights began to melt away. Later, when the sub-way trains started to discharge hordes of commuters, the atmosphere of the place would change completely—a lively, seething river of humanity would course through.

Ananth stopped at a coffee shop under the Toronto-Dominion centre and ordered a double-double and a toasted bagel. When he set down his tray on one of the many deserted tables, he heard a familiar voice greet him: "*Sat Sri Akal!*"

It was Karnail Singh, an old but spry janitor. When Karnail's wife died, he had moved to Canada to live with his son. But, instead of living off his son, Karnail took up the job of a cleaner.

"Sat Sri Akal, *paaji*," Ananth said.

"How are you?" Karnail said. "I don't see you at all, nowadays!"

"Would you like to join me for a cup of coffee?" Ananth said.

"No, thank you."

Ananth knew that Karnail preferred to go back home, after his night shift ended, and have a tall glass of creamy milk with his *makki-di-roti* or some such healthy breakfast.

"Here," Karnail said, tossing a glossy magazine on to the table. "Something for you to read while you're having your coffee." The magazine was in English and was from India. It must have been something left behind by a customer at one of the many restaurants on The Path. It had been a long time since he had set his eyes on an Indian periodical. Ananth avoided anything that had to with India as it stirred uncomfortable emotions within him. Yet he picked up the magazine not to hurt Karnail's feelings, and thumbed through it.

"You look so pale, nowadays," Karnail said. "You almost look like a *firangi*. This lifestyle does not suit you at all. You must get yourself a bride from India."

Karnail loved to talk and offer unsolicited advice to everyone he came across, but he was a friendly and kind-hearted man. "I will, *paaji*, I will," Ananth said absently. Then he saw something in the magazine that made his jaw drop.

"What's the matter, Ananth?" Karnail asked.

"Nothing," Ananth muttered, his mouth full of toasted bagel. "Do you mind if I keep this magazine?"

"Of course not, I'd have thrown it into the garbage any-way," Karnail said, giving a push to his janitor cart. "See you tomorrow, son."

Ananth continued to stare at the magazine spread out on the table in front of him. The page had a garish illustration accompanying the text and the title said, *Born to End-less Night*—a short story by Ananth Diwakar.

* * *

It all started five years before when Ananth was whiling away a lazy Sunday morning, seated on an easy chair in the veranda of his house in Hyderabad and reading the local daily, the *Deccan Chronicle*. As he turned over a page, an advertisement about a seminar on immigration to Canada caught his eye. He decided to attend the seminar and check it out. There was no harm, he told himself, in seeing what it was all about.

Archana, his unprotesting wife, agreed to accompany him. She combed her hair into a tight plait, and wore a gold-bordered silk sari as if they were going to a temple.

Ananth kicked his Vespa to life and wove through the leisurely weekend traffic to a five-star hotel in the Banjara Hills, the venue of the meeting.

In an ice-cold conference room which smelled faintly of mould, they listened to the talk on Canada while biting into sweet-and-salty Osmania biscuits. Ananth was impressed, though the cost seemed a bit too steep. A lesser mortal might have been daunted by the landing fees, the visa charges, and the proof of funds—to say nothing of the consultant's hefty cut. But Ananth was made of sterner stuff—he was an accountant by profession. After returning from the seminar, he spent two days doing sums in his head, while Archana, giving him a wide berth, went around looking like a worried puppy. In his mind, Ananth liquidated his stocks, sold off his scooter, borrowed from Archana's dad (his own dad was a little tight-fisted, and Ananth had very little to do with him) and somehow managed to balance his books. In fact, he showed a surplus of one hundred and fifty rupees.

This was sufficient for Ananth, and he made up his mind then and there to apply for immigration. Though Archana, merely a homemaker, never asked him why he wanted to leave his home and migrate to a cold and faraway land, Ananth somehow felt he was duty-bound to give her an explanation.

"I slog from morning till night, and look how little I make! In India, to buy a small fridge one has to set aside money for years. I bought the used Vespa taking a soft loan from your father.

Archana looked a little wary, but said: "I know what you mean."

"And that's not the only thing," Ananth said. "You know how much I want to be a writer. You've seen for yourself how difficult it is to get an article published. In India, there are no opportunities at all."

"I agree," Archana said.

"Anyone with real talent is not appreciated at all. I want to put my talents to use. I ... I ... want to—"

"You want to find your place in the sun," finished Archana for him. In her mouth the words sounded neither corny nor mocking. All her life she had been tutored to think that a wife was a mere extension of her husband's life. It was no surprise then that she could echo her husband's thoughts as though it were second nature to her.

That was how it came about that they applied for immigration, and bided their time in a state of excitement that had an underlay of anxiety. But as months passed, their initial enthusiasm slowly petered out, leaving behind a feeling of restlessness.

A couple of years went by before they got the letter from the High Commission asking them to have their medical check-ups done. By then Archana was in the family way. So, Ananth travelled alone to Canada, leaving behind Archana and their newborn son. Ananth named him Bharat, after the founder of India—perhaps succumbing to an advance intimation of nostalgia.

When he landed in Toronto, he moved into a guest-house run by a Gujarati couple. A friend whose "co-brother" had stayed there when he went to Canada had recommended the place.

A month later, he rented a room which cost four hundred dollars a month. The amount he had raised in India was considered a small fortune there, but here in Canada it proved to be of little account. It was absolutely imperative that he find himself a job, and quickly, too.

Even as he was mailing out his resumes, Ananth sent out the stories he had written to Canadian magazines and journals. Not one of them was accepted and often he never received a reply. Thinking the South-Asian editors would be more sympathetic, he sent samples of his articles which had appeared in insignificant magazines in India to them. He had hoped they would like them enough to commission him to write for their magazines—there seemed to be so many of them, and could be found stacked at the entrance of every Indian grocery store for free distribution. As usual, there were no takers.

On a computer at the library, he typed out a small piece about a street in Toronto that had the nickname of "Little India." He sent out the 1,000-word article to the *Mississauga News*. It was no surprise when he drew a blank.

The only person who read anything he wrote was Archana. She always replied to his emails promptly. She tried to help him in every way she could. But of what use was her help in a far off country like Canada?

Dear Archie
I haven't found a job as yet. But don't worry; I'm sure something will click. It is only a matter of time. I've made friends with some guys who are from Hydera-bad. They promised to help me. One of them is Satya Prakash. He happens to be a relative of the Bhushans, your dad's friends.

> *How's Bharat? Give him a dozen kisses from me.*
> *The moment I get a job I'll sponsor your immigration.*
> *With love,*
> *Ananth*

One day he was on his way to the central library to give his resume a makeover before he went to visit a security firm in downtown Toronto when he stepped off the bus at Square One in Mississauga. He noticed a thirty-something white woman standing at the bus stop. She was dipping into the various compartments of her handbag, while the other passengers walked around her to board the bus. Without thinking, Ananth pulled out the bus transfer he had on him and offered it, as if it were a rose, to the woman.

She looked at him uncomprehendingly.

"Take it," Ananth said. "With my compliments."

"Er ... I don't think I should," she said, even as she took the bus transfer gingerly, as if it had thorns.

"Don't waste your time thanking me," Ananth said. "The bus is about to leave."

"Oh!" As she was climbing into the bus she said: "I don't know what I did with my transfer ... Thanks!" The door closed with a loud hiss, and the bus peeled away from the curb.

At the library Ananth redrafted his resume to suit a security guard's profile. After making copies of the resume, he took a bus to the subway station. He paid the fare, dropping the coins into a collection box as if paying Charon for a ride to the underworld. As he approached the stairwell, a rather plump young woman who looked like a flyblown version of Meg Ryan was riding up the escalator towards him. When she came closer, he recognized her as the woman to whom he had given the transfer in the morning. She had a collection of plastic carry bags in her hands, and yet was desperately rooting about in her handbag again. She almost stumbled at the landing. She stopped and looked up at Ananth.

He held up the transfer which he had plucked from the dispensing machine, and said: "Will this be of any help to you?"

"It's you, again," she said and laughed. "Have you been stalking me?"

"My name's Ananth," he said, extending his hand.

Unthinkingly she extended her hand, saying: "I'm—" One of the bags she was holding slipped out of her hands and a quantity of small cans fell noisily on to the floor. They rolled away helter-skelter, getting in the way of the scurrying commuters. Ananth went down on all fours and began to retrieve them, as a multitude of legs filed past him. He got up and handed over the tins—mostly pet food—to her. "Here you are!"

"Thank you so much!" she said. "I'm Janis—I was going to buy myself a coffee. Can I get you one?"

"I'd love that."

"Are you from India?"

"Yes," he said. "How did you guess?"

"I spent a couple of months in India," she said as they moved to a teashop run by a Chinese couple. "But it was a long time ago."

As they were sipping their double-double, she said: "When I was in the university I spent a summer backpacking through Asia. In India I went to those shrines in the Hima-layas and the *ashrams* down south, in search of something that was unattainable anyways. But it was great fun while it lasted. Tell me about yourself. What do you do?"

"Much the same thing. Searching for something that's unattainable. In my case, a job."

"I've heard it's hard for immigrants these days," she said.

"You know what," Ananth said with bitterness palpable in his voice, "it is far easier to attain Nirvana, than to get a decent job in Canada."

"What kind of work are you looking for?"

"Any kind! Any survival job, it doesn't matter." He took a look at his watch and added: "I should leave now. I have an appointment downtown. I'm trying for a security guard's job."

"I wish you all the best," Janis said. "In case you don't get the job, let me know. You wouldn't mind working in a shop or a restaurant, would you?"

"I've stopped being fussy long ago."

"Here's my telephone number."

* * *

One week later, Ananth rang up Janis, wondering whether she'd remember him. She not only remembered him but called him over to dine with her on the following Friday.

Janis lived in an apartment block downtown connected to the subway station by an underground passage. She opened the door and welcomed Ananth with the enthusi-asm of an old friend, bussing him on his cheek. Ananth, overcome with shyness, merely said: "Hi!"

The apartment was crammed with bric-a-brac Janis had picked up from the various countries she had visited: bronzes from India, wind-chimes from China, prints from Thailand, wooden dolls from Japan.

"*Cheri*, meet my friend," Janis said. Something on the mantelshelf stirred. It was a large cat totally black except for a generous daub of white on its face. He rubbed his whiskers lazily with his paw, and then slid down from his perch. And bounding up to Janis, he leaped into her hands.

"This is Pondicherry," Janis said.

"Hi," Ananth said to the cat, "you have an unusual name."

Pondicherry gazed at him with his bright, aqueous eyes. He emitted a meow and then looked away, as if enough was enough.

"He is my friend, philosopher and guide," Janis said.

"Now I understand. I have visited Aurbindo's ashram, but merely as a tourist, I'm afraid."

"Shouldn't matter," Janis said, tickling Pondicherry's head. "We are all travellers, one way or the other."

"As an immigrant, I second that."

"That reminds me. What about the security guard's job you had applied for? Did you get it?"

"No such luck. Only the guys with cars got the jobs."

"It must be pretty frustrating. But don't let that get you down." She added cheerfully: "I'm out of work, too. That makes two of us. Tell me, what would you like to drink? I've wine and beer."

Ananth helped himself to a can of beer. Janis filled a tulip with wine.

"Cheers!" Ananth said. "To our blessed state of joblessness."

There was an assortment of chairs and ottomans in the room. Ananth parked his behind on an ottoman, and was startled when he sank almost neck deep into it.

"That's broken," Janis said. "Grab another."

Ananth moved his bottom to the chair beside the ottoman. The stereo was on and strains of oriental music were wafting up like frankincense.

"Do you like Ravi Shankar's music?" Janis said.

"No, I'm not into Indian classical music," he said, taking a deep draught of the beer.

Janis chatted happily all through the evening. She was well-travelled, and had many interests—arcane stuff like Yoga, I Chin and Haiku. Ananth for his part was so fixated on job search that he could only recount his misadventures at the various employment agencies he had visited.

"What made you come to Canada?" Janis asked.

"Looking back, I'd say foolishness," Ananth said, taking a sip of his third Heineken. "But when we applied, we were thinking of the opportunities, quality of life and what not."

"It's hard when you are new. But things will improve, believe me. Once your family comes over, you'll feel a lot better."

"That seems like some distant dream."

"Do you miss your family?"

"Dreadfully."

"Tell me about them."

"I've have son. He's almost a year old now."

He fished out a small photograph from his wallet and showed it to Janis. It was portrait of a mother and child: a young woman with a shy smile was holding a baby who was staring directly into the camera.

"Your son is so much like you! And your wife's so beautiful."

"Yeah," Ananth said, taking back the photo. "Archana is a very quiet, shy person."

"I'm just the opposite; everyone says I talk too much," Janis said, finishing what was left of her wine in one go. "When is your family planning to come to Canada?"

"They will come as soon as I can get a good job. But it doesn't seem any time soon."

"Don't be such a pessimist," said Janis. "Shall we have something to eat?"

She got up unsteadily and went into the tiny kitchen. He heard the door of the microwave pop open and then slam shut. The oven hummed for a few minutes before it started beeping. Janis came back, holding a dish in each hand. She placed them on a low glass-topped Japanese table.

"Would you like another beer?" she asked.

"No," Ananth said, seating himself on a cushion set on the floor. Leaning forward, he began to eat. He found the meat a little too chewy but it was mercifully spicy.

They finished their dinner and were clearing the table when Janis said: "Stop looking at your watch."

"It's getting late. I don't want to miss my bus."

"If I had a car I'd have dropped you home," she said. "My license was revoked last year."

"For what?"

"Drunk driving."

Janis came up close to him. She said: "You can stay here if you want to."

As Ananth took her in his arms, he was dizzied by the perfume she wore. Janis kissed him on his lips.

"What scent you are wearing?" Ananth said.

"Poison."

* * *

Janis must have joked about the perfume because Ananth never found one with that name when he moved into her apartment for good the following week. Janis was living on dole and Ananth was hardly making any money. "Let's join forces," Janis had said. She was good company and generous, and the canny accountant in him noted that he wouldn't have to pony up four hundred dollars every month for rent. Ananth had at last found someone in Canada to champion him, and he felt triumphant.

But as he sat in front of the computer in Janis' flat, looking at the four unopened emails from Archana, he didn't feel that jubilant.

> *I don't see why you have to get so worried* (he wrote in reply to one of Archana's emails). *Everything is fine with me. I have been very busy as I have had to move to another place that costs less. I don't have a job as yet. But I'm looking around.*

After sending the email, Ananth was overcome with a feeling of self-loathing. He knew he was behaving like a heel.

* * *

Janis had an easygoing nature, ready to give and forgive. But Ananth detected a streak of level headedness in her.

Using her network of friends, she found him a job as a helper
at a gift shop in The Path. When he began to earn money,
she expected him to contribute his share of the rent. Ananth was slightly put out at first with this arrangement.

> *I have a job now* (Ananth wrote to Archana). *But I
> am unable to save much money. Sorry about the delay
> in replying to you. I'm very busy at my work and don't
> find so much free time.*

But it was true that he wasn't able to put aside any money.
Whatever he and Janis received as income, they splurged on
parties and merrymaking. Either Janis' friends were always
dropping in, or the two of them were going to some bash or
the other, taking a bottle of quaintly-named wine or big
bowl of tropical-looking salad.

One day, while seated on a bus on the way to a party,
with his arm around Janis' shoulder, Ananth noticed a
young South Asian man in a security guard's garb climb
aboard. Ananth felt something like a kick within his chest.
It can't be Satya! thought Ananth, even as he was hastily
pulling back his arm that was around Janis. He remembered
that Satya was an engineer by profession—surely he couldn't
be working as a security guard?

As he came up the aisle, the young man stopped and
said: "Hi Ananth, how are you doing?"

"Hi, Satya," Ananth said, as he sat awkwardly, his arm
only half-disentangled from Janis.

"You look surprised," Satya said. "Is it my uniform? In
Canada, one has to take up any job that comes one's way."

"No," Ananth said hoarsely. "I'm not surprised."

Satya's eyes strayed to Janis, but quickly darted back to Ananth. "See you later," he said and walked to the back of the bus, losing himself amongst the straphangers.

"You look disturbed," Janis said. "Is he from your country?"

"Yes. From Hyderabad, too."

"Did you know him when you were in India?"

"No, I met him here in Toronto. But we have a few common friends back home."

* * *

One evening, on returning from work, Ananth forced himself to open his Internet mailbox, something he had not done for many weeks. He had been telling himself that he was busy and found no time; whatever the reason, he had steadfastly steered clear of the computer. In the inbox, he found half a dozen messages from Archana. Unopened, unanswered. As he tried to go through them an oppressive feeling came over him. Clicking on the "Reply" button, he began to write:

> *Hi Archie,*
> *Forgive me for not replying earlier. I've been very, very busy at work. I'm doing fine. How are you? How is Bharat—*

He couldn't go on. He didn't enjoy lying to Archana. Even as he sat there, he remembered how Satya had caught him out, red handed as it were. Abruptly he closed the screen and got up.

He made a resolution to write a long email to Archana the following Sunday, to explain—explain what?—and patch up things. But when the weekend came, his resolve deserted him and he put off the unpalatable task to the next weekend. And this went on for a few weeks.

As for Janis, of late she had become edgy and irritable. Ananth couldn't understand what had come over her. She was being impatient not only with him but with Pondicherry too. But at least with Pondicherry, Ananth noticed, she'd try to make amends.

"No worries," Janis said one day, in a voice that betrayed a great deal of worry. "There's a month to go before they stop my EI payments. I'll find myself a job by then."

One evening when he got back from late from work, he found Janis in a celebratory mood. The stereo was playing rock and she had opened a bottle of champagne. She actually had a smile on her face, something Ananth had not seen in a long time.

"I've got good news!" she yelled out. "I found a job. I'm going to teach English in South Korea."

"South Korea!" Ananth said, aghast. He recovered and added: "That's awesome."

"Can I leave Pondicherry behind and trust you to take care of him? I'll only be away for a year."

Ananth felt a little peeved that she was not asking him to accompany her but, on second thought, he was comforted that she was treating him on par with Pondicherry.

"When do you have to go?"

"Soon," she said. "By the end of the month."

The vein of common sense Janis possessed surfaced once more. She completed all the formalities so that Ananth could continue to live in the flat. When the time came for

Janis to leave for Pusan, she handed Pondicherry to Ananth and said: "I'll be back, soon, my pets. Take care!"

After Janis' departure, there was a lull in Ananth's life. He felt not only lonely but let down too. There were times when he wished he could sink into the earth, like a worm, and disappear forever from the world. By and by he got used to his single life and even began to enjoy his privacy and solitude. He chucked the job he had in the gift shop and took up another one at a shop that sold cell phones. Not only was the pay better, he felt more comfortable working there—he had stuck out like sore thumb at "Lovin' & Givin'."

Though his new place of work was farther away than the gift shop, it was still on The Path. Whether it rained or snowed, he could always get to work in relative comfort. Besides, on his way back from work he could buy all the things he needed. He began to live like a gnome, almost never feeling the urge to go out into the open world. On the rare occasion he stepped outside, he invariably encountered something that would make him bolt back double quick.

Like the day he was having a drink in a patio, sitting by the roadside and watching the world pass by.

"Hi," a voice said. It was Kumar. Also known as The Prince, he had been one of the houseguests at the place Ananth had checked into after arriving in Canada.

"You're the guy from Hyderabad, aren't you, who wanted to become a writer?" Kumar said.

"Yeah," Ananth said, gritting his teeth.

"Have you written anything lately?"

"No. It's not easy to get your stuff published in Canada."

"Nothing is easy here, my friend. Let me tell you that. You must enrol at one of the writing courses. I heard Hunger College has an excellent program."

"Thanks for the tip. I believe the name is Humber."
Hunger College, indeed! No wonder so many writers starve
to death.

"How's your family?" The Prince asked. "Have you
brought them over from India?"

It appeared to Ananth that Kumar's eyes were watching
him closely.

"No," Ananth said, drinking up the contents of his
glass in one big gulp. He set down the glass on the table and
abruptly took leave of The Prince.

After that he was reluctant to leave the confines of The
Path. He felt somehow secure in its labyrinthine underbelly.
And the long walks on The Path seemed to be doing him
good.

His new-found loneliness also made him flirt with the
idea of going back to writing. Secretly he had always seen
himself as a best-selling author writing under the name of
Akash Dewan—a pseudonym catchy and modern, unlike
his own name. On his long walks in The Path, the persona
of Akash Dewan would often take over and many a plot for
short stories entered his head. But in the end it never came
to anything. When Ananth actually sat down in front of the
monitor to write, whatever creative urge he had felt evaporated in a blink. The computer reminded him of all the unanswered emails from Archana.

* * *

When Ananth finished reading the story in the magazine
Karnail Singh had given him, he was at once seized with a
feeling of triumphant joy. At long last somebody somewhere
had found his story worthy of publication. It wasn't an easy

matter to have a story published in India, or anywhere else for that matter, as he had found out the hard way.

Ananth turned a page and came upon a review of *Diwakar's Dozen*—a book supposedly written by him. So it was not just one story but a whole book of them that was published. Apparently, there were 13 stories in the collection. Ananth was stupefied; as far as he remembered he had written only nine, and two of those were incomplete.

He noticed a box item in a corner that contained a short interview with the author. The fact that there was no photograph of the author was not lost upon Ananth.

Interviewer: Ananth, the content and style of your stories vary a lot. Let us take *Born to Endless Night* and *A Mouthful of Sherry*. The former is a gritty story of rural poverty in India and the latter is an airy pastiche of Sherlock Holmes. They are not only so different from each other, they might have been written by two very different writers. How do you explain that?

Diwakar: I wrote some of these stories a long time ago. Since I couldn't find a publisher they were put into cold storage. Times change and I've changed too over the years, and these things tell on your output, you know. Besides, I love the detective story and on a whim I wrote the parody on the most famous detective.

Ananth had no love for the detective story; he was a devotee of horror novels. Was Archana writing under his name? Ananth found that hard to believe; Archana had graduated in a subject called "Home Science," if you please. She wasn't particularly fond of reading though he had found her occasionally with an Agatha Christie. But then why didn't she write her so called pastiche on Poirot or Miss Marple? Why Holmes?

Archana must have taken a lot of pains to have that book published. How had she managed it? How was she managing with her life? Of course, her Dad was always there to help her out. And Bharat! He must be nearly four now.

How had they reacted to his disappearance from their lives? He had left for Canada, and then fallen off the map altogether. How worried Archana must have felt at the beginning, not knowing what had become of him. Her father, though well off by Indian standards, wouldn't have had the resources to start a manhunt for him. Maybe he wrote to the High Commission, but it was more probable he contacted his friends with connections in Canada. Like Satya.

Ananth got up from the chair and went to the alcove that housed the home computer. He opened his Internet mailbox and scrolled all the way down. He saw many unread mails form Archana. He opened the last mail from her and found that it was dated two years ago. He discovered his half-written letter still sitting in the "draft" folder. On an impulse he sent it. Even as he was seated at the computer, the mail bounced back, undelivered.

He called his home number in Hyderabad. After six tries, a thin reedy voice told him in Telugu that the number was not in service. The next morning on his way to work, he stopped at the ATM in the Royal Bank Building and checked his account balance. He had fourteen hundred and fifty seven dollars. On his way back he booked a passage to India.

When he returned to the apartment that night, Pondicherry leaped down from his lair on the mantelpiece and tried to shinny up Ananth's legs, purring all the while. The cat had never been so effusive in his welcome before.

"Hello, old boy," Ananth said. "You will have to be on your own for a few days. I hope you will not mind."

On the day he was leaving for India, Ananth put Pondicherry into a cage that looked like a lady's vanity case but with vents cut into them. He took the cat over to Karnail Singh's place; Pondicherry was mewling all the while.

"I'll be back soon," Ananth said to Pondicherry.

"Tell him not to return alone," Karnail said. "He should come back with a wife."

"I will," Ananth said. "I promise you."

* * *

After disembarking in Hyderabad, he changed some of his dollars into Indian Rupees and joined a long queue for an auto-rickshaw.

The traffic on the road was light, but there were dozens of pedestrians, out for their morning constitutional. The early morning air was cool and bracing, but once sun began to move up the sky, it would become quite hot. The city looked beautiful with its shimmering lakes and rock-studded hills. Truly, a place in the sun, a place he had turned his back on.

When the auto-rickshaw turned into the familiar lane where his house stood, Ananth felt a heaviness in his chest. The driver stopped in front of a wrought-iron gate. Ananth got out of the auto-rickshaw, and paid the driver. He pushed open the gate and walked up the short drive. The lantana bushes on either side needed pruning and the patch of lawn in front of the small portico was browned here and there by the topical sun.

As he approached the house he noticed that the maid-servant had already swept the front yard and had adorned the patch of ground in front of the main door with a *moggu* —a geometric pattern of dots and lines made with rice flour.

The front door was open and the soft strains of a *bhajan* played on a tape-recorder wafted towards him. There was nobody about. He could smell the unmistakable fragrance of sandalwood incense sticks. In the verandah, there were two easy-chairs and a child's tricycle. On a writing table at the far end there was a photograph—a studio portrait of a child flanked by two adults. The smiling child must be Bharat. One of the adults was Archana and the other was a man Ananth had never seen before.

He checked his impulse to walk in, and instead rang the doorbell. In a few seconds, the curtains leading to the living room parted and a man stepped out. He was the man in the photograph.

"Yes?" he said in English, not in Telugu, not in Urdu. Instinctively the man had known that Ananth did not belong there. Was it the cut of his clothes? His hairstyle?

Ananth was suddenly assailed by a feeling to turn back and go away. But he couldn't leave without saying anything. "I wanted to know how to get in touch with Professor Nagaraj. He was my teacher in the university." That part was true, though theirs had been an arranged marriage, Archana's father had taught him bookkeeping. On retirement, he had returned to his native village, leaving the house for him and Archana to live in.

"He passed away a year ago. He had been ill for a long time."

"Why? What happened?"

"He had cancer of the esophagus. He came back to live here so that he could get medical attention and Archana could take care of him. Can you wait for a few minutes? Archana's in the bathroom. You might want to talk to her."

Casting a glance at Ananth's suitcase, he added: "Why don't you come in? I'll get you a cup of coffee."

"Please don't bother. I'm in a hurry," Ananth said. "By the way, are you the famous writer?"

The man smiled and said: "I'm not sure about being famous, but yes, I'm Ananth Diwakar."

"Pleased to meet you," Ananth said. "I should be leaving now. I have a plane to catch."

As Ananth was walking away, the man said: "You've not told me your name."

Ananth stopped in his tracks and, looking at the man squarely in the eye, said: "Akash Dewan."

Ananth walked to the main road, so deep in thought that he looked as if was furiously doing sums in his head. Archana's father would have got his abandoned daughter re-married, afraid she would be alone with a small child in this world, with no one to take care of them once he passed on. Who was the man? Was he one of the professor's old students? Or someone Archana mevt when she was trying to get his stories published? Or was he an old classmate of hers he had never heard about?

The loud bellow of an auto-rickshaw interrupted his thoughts—and he flagged it down.

"Where do you want to go, *saar*?" the driver asked.

Where should he go? Was there any place he would like to go back to? Was there anyone who wanted him?

"Pondicherry!" he said.

"What are you saying, *saar*? How can I take you to Pondicherry in my auto? Do you want me to take you to a railway station?"

"No," Ananth said. "Take me to the airport."

Ananth knew what he would do when he got back to Toronto. He would give writing another shot—as Akash Dewan. He was sure he would be quite good at plotting stories with a twist at the end.

Acknowledgements

I thank the Art Councils of Mississauga and Ontario respectively for the award and grant bestowed on me. I am indebted to the support extended by 'Diaspora Dialogues' in a variety of ways and for so many years. I am grateful to Todd Cloutier, Amy Ferguson and Sheila Czernkovich who are (or were) with Great West Life, my employer, for encouraging me in my literary pursuits as well.

While I cannot thank here all my friends who believed in me, I would like to put on record my gratitude to Ada Zimmermann, Aparna Rayaprol, Arunesh Maiyar, Cheryl Xavier, Gita Srikantan, Jasmine D'Costa, Nuzhat Abbas, and Satyam Pothamsetty.

Last but not least, I'd like to thank my publishers Michael Mirolla and Connie McParland of Guernica Editions, and Sam Brown my editor for helping make an immigrant's dream a reality.

About The Author

Pratap Reddy moved to Canada from India in 2002. An underwriter by day and a writer by night, he writes about the angst and the agonies (on occasion the ecstasies) of newly arrived immigrants. His stories have been published in Canada, India, and the USA. He is working on a second volume of short fiction, and a novel. He lives in Mississauga with his wife and son.

MARQUIS

Québec, Canada

RECYCLED
Paper made from
recycled material
FSC® C103567

Printed on Enviro 100% post-consumer EcoLogo certified paper,
processed chlorine free and manufactured using biogas energy.